Devil's Daughter

JANE PEARCE

Order this book online at www.trafford.com
or email orders@trafford.com

Most Trafford titles are also available at major online book retailers.

© Copyright 2019 Jane Pearce.
All rights reserved. No part of this publication may be reproduced, stored in a retrieval
system, or transmitted, in any form or by any means, electronic, mechanical, photocopying,
recording, or otherwise, without the written prior permission of the author.

Print information available on the last page.

ISBN: 978-1-4907-9299-6 (sc)
ISBN: 978-1-4907-9298-9 (hc)
ISBN: 978-1-4907-9300-9 (e)

Library of Congress Control Number: 2019930217

Because of the dynamic nature of the Internet, any web addresses or links contained
in this book may have changed since publication and may no longer be valid. The views
expressed in this work are solely those of the author and do not necessarily reflect the
views of the publisher, and the publisher hereby disclaims any responsibility for them.

Any people depicted in stock imagery provided by Getty Images are models, and such images
are being used for illustrative purposes only.
Certain stock imagery © Getty Images.

Trafford rev. 01/03/2019

www.trafford.com
North America & international
toll-free: 1 888 232 4444 (USA & Canada)
fax: 812 355 4082

Chapter 1

The first snowfall of winter is usually a joyful time in the city of Harmon. What were once dark, dingy streets are now covered in a fresh layer of bright, clean snow. The sad faces on the souls struggling through life now show signs of happiness, contentment, and hope. The excitement and rush of walking over a fresh layer of snow with each individual snowflake being completely different feels almost magical. Most people consider human beings to be a lot like snowflakes, completely different and unique. Abby knew different. Through the fake smiles, everyone had a dark side, a side that was so visible to her that it made her sick. Sometimes Abby would go days without leaving her apartment except to work, which, luckily for her, was Duffy's, the small local pub just across the street from her apartment building. Her boss and the owner of Duffy's, Liz, was the only person Abby could even stand to be around for any long periods. Liz had given Abby employment at a difficult time. They were both desperate and benefited each other's lives. It was shallow, but it was also the most stable relationship Abby could cling to right now.

It began like most days for Abby. She had worked her usual shift until closing time. The cold morning air coming in the open windows filled the tiny one-room apartment with shivering temperatures. It was the perfect sleeping condition, especially for someone naturally overheated. Abby had the only bachelor apartment in her building. The rest of the apartments were much more expensive, which made this one of the few decent buildings left with mostly older people who want a quiet place. And it usually was. Abby began to wake as the dark red curtains blew just softly enough that they provided a calming white noise. It's too bad comfort is usually short-lived. A loud knock forced Abby out of her calmed state. She flipped a red blanket off her face, revealing a look of frustration. Sleeping wasn't something to be taken for granted anymore. As she got to her feet, she took a moment to close the windows and curtains. Everyone always thought she was a little odd for not liking the sun, among other reasons. She held onto a small end table for a moment to let her eyes adjust. Her hand accidentally knocked over a candle burning from the night before. The dried wax still smelled of vanilla. As she made her way to check the peephole, she fell over her boots she had forgotten to put away yet again.

"Shit!" she shouted, just loud enough for a male on the other side of the door to answer.

"You all right in there?"

Abby got her back up, holding on to the small counter area with a sink that was supposed to be considered a kitchen.

"Fine," she said.

She grunted in anger as she reached the door. It was the police— again. This was the third time this week they had gone around knocking on doors in that area. It was the same one she had ignored before—tall, blond hair, blue eyes, typical innocent look, perfect to get people to trust him and open up. But behind those blue eyes were some blackened thoughts. As Abby decided whether to open the door, the detective started to look as though he was rushed and moved on to her neighbor's head. He knocked loudly again, this time loud enough to fill the hallway with his presence. Abby listened as a woman answered the door. Her voice was soft and aged. In all the time Abby lived there, she never once introduced herself. She greeted the officer kindly.

"May I help you?" she offered with excitement. Abby smirked. Her decision not to meet the upbeat morning person was validated.

"I'm Detective Deeks. I'm investigating a string of suspicious fires in the area." He continued. "Would you be able to confirm your whereabouts between the hours of three and four o'clock this morning?"

Abby lifted her face away from the door and put her hands up to her mouth in shock. That was the time she was walking home from work. It was just across the street, but the crime was so bad lately that even that was a dangerous walk. She remembered saying goodbye to Liz in the parking lot and watching her drive away in her little rusted-out car. Then she walked into the Busy Market right after work to grab some things she needed before going home and locking herself away from society. She decided to grab something to drink, and some men approached her, and then she was in bed but calm, so calm, the calmest she had been since. *Oh crap,* Abby thought with worry. *I think the blackouts are getting worse.*

Like everything else that went wrong in her life, Abby decided to try and ignore the problems going on in the world surrounding her and, lately, even her own problems. She slipped out of her robe and walked into the bathroom. Abby leaned over and started the hot water first. Her fiery red hair was finally released from the braid from the night before as she massaged her scalp. The steam coming off her pale skin fogged up the mirror almost instantly. As she was rinsing the conditioner out of her long red locks, another knock echoed through her apartment, bouncing off the shower walls.

"Shit, this place used to be so quiet!" she snapped sarcastically with no one around to hear, just as she liked it. She darted out of the shower and slipped her robe back on, her hair still dripping wet. As she rushed over to the door, another knock echoed from the other side. This time it wasn't the same detective, but he still looked like one. A tall man with an intimidating posture was on the door with a knock that a deaf turtle would respond to.

"Can I help you?" she shouted defensibly through her door.

"My name's Ryan Finney. I'm moving in across the hall," he explained.

Abby waited for him to go on as an awkward silence crept over them. "And!" she snapped finally.

Ryan replied, "And I was hoping I could wait in your place until the superintendent gets here."

"Sorry!" Abby yelled. "I'm busy, and I'm not stupid!"

She stormed away from the door after putting the dead bolt on it. A single woman letting a complete stranger into her home was even stupid for someone who could take care of themselves. Just another neighbor she'd have to avoid. It took her months to get rid of Michelle. Michelle had moved across the hall around the same time Abby had just settled into her place two years ago. The only problem was that Michelle was a typical eighteen-year-old at the time. It was her first time away from home, and she needed friendship and company. She would constantly be at the door, wanting to hang around Abby's place. Abby had lived on her own since she was fourteen. Her mother was a violent alcoholic, and her father's situation was complicated. She wanted silence and solitude to keep her calm, not constant hounding.

"I'm not some creep! I just don't have the keys yet! He should be here within the hour!" he shouted into the door.

Abby ignored his words and closed the bathroom door. The sound of the shower covered up his pleas perfectly. The morning was finally back on track.

As Abby got dressed, her mind wandered as usual. Her phone began to ring.

She answered, "Hello?"

The other end responded with an overly enthusiastic customer service tone, "Hello, Abby! This is Dr. Robert's office. I'm just calling to remind you about your anger management counseling session today. Please try and make this one. The last two cancellations were very short notice."

Abby hung up the phone without replying. "I hate these appointments! All they do is cause more anger and frustration!" she snapped.

Regardless, Abby started getting ready to head out. The rip in the knee of her jeans was covered by the thigh-high, jet-black boots she always wore out of habit. Her tank top was covered with a cheap but awesome fake leather jacket that was fitted to her body. As she locked her door and headed toward the road, she decided to grab some gum for the trip at the Busy Market. Once she got to the corner, the scene was a mess. The Busy Market was gone, completely burned to the ground. The area was cut off by yellow caution tape, but a crowd was still there just on the outside of the taped-off area, looking at the crime scene. A young woman who looked very upset made eye contact with Abby.

"Do you know what happened?" Abby asked.

"No one knows," the young girl replied. "The police say two men are dead and only the owner of the store got out alive."

Abby quickly walked away. *I was just there!* she thought. The whole way to her appointment, she ran scenarios in her head about how things could have gone differently or how she could have been killed. It seemed selfish even to her, but the timing was just crazy. Harmon was getting even worse for crime, if that was possible.

Abby arrived at the office a few minutes late and checked in. A young man was behind the desk. His hair was riddled with grease buildup, and his skin was broken out and oily. He sat slouched over, not paying attention to his surroundings. When she walked in, he was texting. She took advantage of this and sat without making a noise, hoping she wouldn't have to speak to him.

"Yo, you know you're late, right?" he snapped at her without looking up from his phone.

"Yo?" she replied. "I'm late because there was another fire near my apartment building."

The greaseball finally looked up from his phone. The name tag "Darrell" was covered in stains and something she hoped was mayonnaise. The look and his tone were enough to set her off. Abby

5

stood and walked over to the counter. She leaned over it, staring down at him in his chair.

"Darrell, is it?" Abby said with an eerie, crooked smile on her face. "Darrell, can you tell me why the people who work here are either so overly positive that they shit sugar or they're like . . . you." Darrell stared at her, confused. "Tell the doc I quit. I'd much rather live with my anger than put up with this each week."

She grabbed her bag and slammed the door behind her. Abby was baffled that an anger management center would hire someone so anger-triggering to actually greet the patients. It was a miracle he hadn't gotten his neck snapped yet. Abby looked back for a moment at the office, so tempted to go back and do something violent. But once again, she swallowed this urge, an urge that kept building until she could let loose.

Walking down the street never used to be so dangerous. Most decent people had already moved out of Harmon and into smaller towns outside the city. The streets were now filled with gang members and thieves. Assaults were now a regular occurrence, and because of the volume, it was unlikely the cops could ever make it there to help. Women never walked down the streets alone except for Abby. Not caring whether you live or die really took away any fear for your safety. It was almost freeing—in an extremely morbid kind of way, of course. The homeless people were no longer just sitting on the streets begging. They actively took what they wanted and would leave you for dead if you refused.

Shortly before Abby was born, Harmon had such a bright future. The lakes surrounding it had many metal factories on them, bringing jobs and attracting many working-class people. But that was twenty years ago. All but one of those factories were gone now. And they barely kept any staff as it was. It's amazing what two decades can do to a community. Abby continued noticing the depressing streets as she walked on toward home after dealing with that office.

An emergency radio and TV broadcast took over the streets. On a storefront TV, the chief of police, Charles Doyle, prepared to address his city.

"At this time, a mandatory curfew will be put in place while separate investigations are ongoing and crime rate continues to rise. Employers will have work permits for you if your hours are within the curfew. You must keep this on you and present it when an officer requests."

As soon as the initial statement finished, hysteria followed as people ran through the streets and fled to their homes. Abby stood there as people ran around her, bumping into her and fleeing.

"We are urging the public not to panic," Chief Doyle finished.

Abby laughed. "I guess he should have started with that," she said out loud to herself.

The streets got louder. The announcements could no longer be heard as the panic worsened. Abby continued down the street, her apartment building approaching on the left. She got to the apartment door and flung it open, knocking over a fake plant with the force. She took a moment to pick it. Layers of dust and neglect rubbed off on her hands. *Gross,* she thought.

Abby had got home and flung her jacket over her bed. She took her bra off and tossed it onto the bed as well. She looked down and said softly, "Sorry, girls, that one was cruel." She held her breasts while she walked. She took a moment and looked at her phone—seven missed calls from Liz. "Come on, Liz, it's my day off," huffed Abby.

This affected her, this, not the panic on the streets but possibly getting called into work. Now that was an annoyance to Abby. The eighth call came rolling in. Abby looked at the phone, deciding to answer. She held it in one hand and continued to massage the pain of the day with the other.

She answered, "Hel—"

"Abby!" Liz shouted, cutting her off. "Abby, have you heard?"

"Yeah, I was outside when he made the announcement," Abby replied.

"I need you to work tonight. None of the other girls are willing to go out on the streets," Liz begged.

Abby paused. "I want time and a half," she said before slamming the phone down, playing hard to get.

Of course, she would get it. The gangs were whining; everyone was scared. Instead of having the night to herself, she now only had an hour of downtime. Abby sat on her small single bed and looked around her apartment, her tiny couch in the corner and the TV she never watched. It wasn't much, but she wished she never had to leave it and deal with the real world. She lay down and stared at her ceiling. It was clean, but that was the nicest thing about it. Like everything else about that building, it was dull, so plain that maybe Abby could even blend in. A text alert made her look back down at her phone. It was from Liz. It read,

Thank you so much!

It didn't matter how ill-mannered Abby may be. Liz always accepted her, or needed her. To Abby, there wasn't a difference. Abby grabbed her phone and lay back down. She set her alarm and decided to try and get some more sleep before her surprise shift tonight. She covered herself with her favorite high thread count bright red sheet. The material was perfect and let her naturally warm skin breathe.

The pub was pretty dead that night. Abby came in and noticed that she was the first to track any of the new fallen snow in. That was definitely not a good sign for business.

"It's going to be an early night tonight. The other waitresses quit again," Liz said as Abby took off her coat and grabbed her apron.

Abby rolled her eyes. No customers meant no tips. Abby budgeted perfectly for the job she had. She paid her rent and phone with her paycheck and used the tip money for anything extra. She lived day by day, and this worked for her up until now.

"Is there any prep work that needs to be done?" Abby asked, trying to stay busy.

"I've been doing it. There's nothing else to do. I haven't even had to turn on the grill today," said Liz as she sat in a booth. "I made us a pizza. Should be done soon," said Liz.

"Thanks!" said Abby. "I'm starving."

Liz smiled. "At least I get to cook for someone today."

Two full hours went by without any foot traffic into the restaurant. Liz came out of the kitchen and offered Abby a platter of mixed appetizers she had put together.

"Thanks!" said Abby as she sat, allowing Liz to pull her arm. "We need customers soon, or I'm going to get super fat," Abby joked. Liz laughed nervously. "What's wrong?" Abby asked.

"Do you think they'll catch the firebug?" asked Liz. "It happened right after we closed. I can't believe it." She continued.

Abby looked up at Liz. Her skin looked like it aged rapidly since all this began. "I heard they were gang members who died," Abby added.

"That doesn't mean they deserve to be burned alive," expressed Liz.

Abby smiled and nodded in agreement even if it wasn't true. Liz was so innocent. She believed there was good in everyone, so naive. Sometimes it was nice for Abby to hear a calmer perspective on things. The way things were now, it took courage to try and be positive, or delusions. But both could work if you tried hard enough.

The first customer of the night looked oddly familiar, which was extremely unusual since Abby never noticed or really talked to anyone. He came in and sat quietly. As he looked down, his thick dark hair shielded his face. Abby approached him.

"What can I get you?" she asked as she emerged from behind the bar.

"Whatever you have on tap, Ms. 108," he replied.

She stopped and shockingly asked, "Excuse me?"

"Your apartment number," he said with a smirk. "I'm Ryan. I tried to introduce myself earlier today but clearly stepped over the line. I moved across the hall from you."

Abby took a step back. "I don't like people knocking on my door," she said. Ryan looked up at her and continued to smirk. "Let me get that drink for you," Abby awkwardly said as she walked over to the bar and began preparing his order. She finished quickly and rushed back over. "How did you know what I looked like?" she asked, slamming down the glass.

"I just told you. I moved across the hall and recognized you."

"No," replied Abby. "You talked to me through my door. We've never met. How do you know who I am?" she insisted.

"Fine." He sighed. "My name is Det. Ryan Finney. I'm trying to keep my occupation private until we finish investigating the firebug in this area," he said while he played with his utensils.

"So you moved here to spy on the residents? Yeah, no wonder you wouldn't want everyone to find out," she said sarcastically.

"Not only that. I got divorced over a year ago, so this seemed like a good way to start over," he explained.

Abby looked puzzled. "Okay, so since there's no one at home to impress, should I grab the dessert menu?"

Ryan started laughing, to Abby's surprise. They stared at each other for a moment.

"You're definitely unique. What time are you off?" he asked. "You should stop by for a drink. I'm pretty much unpacked and settled in. Makes it easier when the ex-wife keeps everything, including your socks."

Abby gave him a smile and said, "I'll think about it. By the way, I'm Abby, but of course, you already knew that."

Ryan smiled and then reached out and took her hand. "It's a real pleasure to meet you, Abby."

Abby went back to grab his drink. Liz sneaked over, crouching down so as not to be seen. "Who's that?" she said, pointing at Ryan. "He's hot," she added.

"You should take him this then," Abby said as she finished pouring his beer.

"Are you sure?" Liz said with excitement.

But before Abby could answer, she grabbed it and was off chatting with Ryan. Abby went behind the counter and continued Liz's prep work, unaware of Ryan's eyes following her.

The pub lights went out as the door locked. The small back door opened, and Abby closed it firmly behind her. Abby walked across the street and saw that Ryan had still got his lights on. She went directly to her door and closed it behind her. *Thank God*, she thought. All she wanted to do was be alone and relax. But the plans never worked out. Abby turned around, only to find a dark figure standing in her way. It grabbed her by the arm with such pressure it felt like it was breaking. She screamed, and her blood boiled. Her face went visibly red. As she screamed, it flew against the wall as if it were being thrown by the rhythm of her anger. It was a man but not exactly. He was at least seven feet tall with very thick-looking skin, but his face wasn't exactly normal. There was something evil here.

"Abby!" Ryan shouted as he banged on the door. Ryan had heard everything while unpacking across the hall and, within seconds, had kicked in the door. Whatever it was, it was gone. Her window was smashed. "What happened?" he asked.

Abby took a moment to gather herself before answering, "I'm not exactly sure, but he'll be back," she said, sounding defeated. "He always comes back."

Ryan had no idea what was happening or what Abby was talking about. "Well, whoever he is, he's injured." He pointed to a dark-colored blood splatter on the wall. "I'm calling this in, and after they get your statement, you'll be staying at my place tonight."

Abby's normal instinct told her to refuse, but his remarks were untainted by the underlying evil intent that she was so used to experiencing. "I can agree to that," she said, accepting.

"Good," Ryan said. "Let's wait at my place until they get here."

Abby agreed without hesitation. She had other things on her mind. This was the first time anything like this happened without her blacking out. Ryan touched her arm to gently lead her out, and she yelled. She rolled up her sleeve. The bruising was already visible.

"I'm so sorry," he said.

Abby held her arm as they walked. "You didn't do it," she said.

Chapter 2

---

*R*yan's hand protectively touched Abby's waist as he sat with her in his apartment. She hated being touched, but his arm around her felt natural. They sat without speaking for a few moments until Ryan got up. Abby reached for him, to her shock.

"I'm just going to go make a phone call to the police, all right?" he said as he got closer to her. "I'll just be right over there." He pointed to the sliding door that led to a small balcony.

She nodded at him. As she looked around, she noticed awards, medals, and lots of guns. A small shelf on the wall beside the door held frames with pictures of young Ryan and what appeared to be his parents. Many pictures were displayed but only up until a certain age.

"They're on their way," Ryan said, startling Abby. Abby turned around, still holding one of the photos she was looking at. It was a beautiful family photo, him and his mom sitting on a bench at the beach and his dad leaning over them with his arms out. It was a sunny and happy time, a different time. "Can you tell me what happened?" he asked softly.

Abby's mind was too unhinged at the moment to focus on his words. "What happened to your parents?" she asked, bluntly changing the subject. Ryan laughed uncomfortably and ran his hand through his hair awkwardly. Abby held up the family photo and pointed to a little girl standing next to him. "Is this your sister?" she asked.

"Yes," he said as he took the picture gently from her. His index finger traced over his mother's face. "They were killed when I was nine," he confessed.

Abby looked at the photo for a moment. "All of them?" she asked. "By whom?"

Ryan stared at her with amazement that she would ask these questions. "I've never spoken to anyone about this before," he confessed. "Where are your parents?" he asked.

Abby looked at him. "That's fair." She smiled. "My mother is a useless bum that's probably ruining someone else's life somewhere. I've been on my own for a while now."

"And your father?" he asked.

Abby took a moment. "That's not as easy to explain."

Just then, a knock at the door made them both freeze.

"Ryan, it's Phil. Open up."

Ryan got up and went over to the door. As he opened up the door, he motioned at Abby to hold their train of thought, and another detective walked in, the same detective who had been hounding all the residents in her area. His blond hair and blue eyes were unmistakable. He was absolutely flawless, and he seemed to know it. He dressed and acted in a way that didn't leave his womanizing ways a mystery.

"This is my partner, Abby, Phil Deeks," Ryan said.

Phil sat beside Abby. "Hello, Abby. I know you're shaken up, but can you briefly tell me what happened tonight?" He slowly slid closer to her.

Abby was extremely uncomfortable. "I already spoke to Ryan," Abby said, hoping to end the interaction.

"So there's nothing else?" Phil said, placing his hand on Abby's thigh. Abby glared at Phil. Even Ryan's face seemed unamused by this action. She didn't like him, not because of his obvious douchebag demeanor but because he didn't care who was after her. He cared about what he was after. "He was about six feet and wore a hoodie. He was there waiting. I don't know what else to tell you," she lied.

Phil looked at Ryan, a look that made his disbelief obvious. "Why don't we try this again when you've had some time to relax after such an experience?" he suggested with a look of frustration.

Abby looked away. There was something about him she just didn't trust. Ryan stood and showed Phil to the door.

"There's something off about her, Ryan. Do you think she could be connected to the fires in the area?"

Ryan stepped outside and closed the door behind him. "Is that truly what you believe?" he asked in a confrontational manner.

Phil didn't answer but nodded as he put his hands in his pockets and walked down the hallway toward the exit. Ryan entered back into his apartment.

"Your door isn't secure and won't be able to be repaired until tomorrow. You can take the bed."

"I can take the couch," she insisted. "I doubt I'll be sleeping anyway."

Ryan shook his head. "That's not how I do things," he said.

Abby thought about calling Liz to let her know what happened. But it was already late, and she knew Liz would just try feeding her.

As things finally started to calm down, it was getting very late. The sun would soon be up if Abby didn't get to sleep soon. Ryan started the shower and closed the bathroom door. Abby went across the hall to grab a few things she would need for the evening. When she got into her apartment, she noticed how right Ryan was. Her door was barely attached to the hinges. The blood had been cleaned, but the stains remained on the floor and walls. The glass from the window was still lying across the red fabric on her couch. Abby grabbed her broom from the bathroom and began to sweep the glass off the floor first. She carefully picked the glass off the couch as well. Abby noticed the glass had cut a small piece out of her couch. It took her two months to save for this piece of crap, and now this freak got to cut it? This changed her mood from startled to extremely angry.

Abby grabbed a few things from her bathroom and left the wreck of an apartment.

By the time she got back to Ryan's, he was done in the shower, so she went into the bathroom and began to undress as well. It had been such a long day, and a super cold shower would be perfect to cool off her boiling rage. She could hear Ryan's headphones blasting music. He was oblivious to his surroundings and had no idea she had even gotten back from across the hall. He opened the bathroom door, deafened by tunes. Abby screamed loud enough to startle him and covered herself with the shirt she had just taken off.

"I'm so sorry!" Ryan yelled as he covered his eyes. He ran toward the door and hit the wall, knocking a hanging picture off. Glass was shattering all around Abby today, it seemed.

"Just go! I'll get it!" Abby said, hoping it would stop Ryan from stumbling around and breaking something else.

Ryan left with his eyes still covered by one hand as his other arm reached out to feel obstructions in front of him. Abby closed the door. The sound of the glass dragging under the door on the bathroom tiles wasn't pleasant at all. Abby got in and was quick in the shower. Ryan had a typical bachelor's bathroom—barely any products at all, hotel art (until he broke it), and a single towel. It was smart thinking to grab her own stuff.

Pieces of glass hit the garbage can in Ryan's kitchen. Abby had cleaned up the bathroom and gotten dressed. She came out in a red robe wearing black PJ bottoms.

"So did you want to talk more about what happened?" Ryan asked as Abby sat on the opposite end of his couch.

"If you wouldn't mind, I'd actually like to forget about it for the night," she said.

"That's fine. Would you like to watch a movie or something?" Ryan asked.

Abby walked over to the small stand beside his TV. Aside from movies, he had many vintage board games as well. "Where did you get all these?" she asked.

"I've had them ever since I was little," he said, smiling.

Abby picked a game she hadn't seen in forever. "Snakes and ladders!" she said as she brought it over to the coffee table dividing them and sat.

"Are you sure you want to do this? I'm the master," Ryan joked.

Abby opened the box and set up the game. "Then I guess it's only fair I go first," she said, grabbing the dice. And then she rolled, a perfect six.

The morning sun began to creep in the window and dance across Abby's face. She awoke to the smell of freshly brewed coffee filling the apartment. She lifted her legs over the edge of the bed and stood. They had played for hours last night Abby didn't even remember getting into the bed. When Abby got into the bathroom and looked into the mirror, she noticed the smudged makeup from the night before. Abby splashed some water on her face and grabbed some toilet paper. Ruining her towels with makeup was one thing, but normal people hate that. She scrubbed her face, removing all the makeup.

Oh god, he's going to see me without makeup, she thought. *Poor guy.* Abby finished up and dried herself off. After looking around her a while, she noticed that she had forgotten a brush. It took her a while to run her fingers through her hair and tame it. Abby could hear Ryan doing things around the house.

"Ryan, do you have an elastic?" she shouted. A rubber band came shooting through the door and hit Abby right in the ass. "Ow!" she yelled.

"Score!" shouted Ryan.

Abby braided her hair to one side and sealed it with the band. She cleaned up her area and looked in the mirror. A red hue clouded her eyes lately. It looked odd but pretty cool. Every time she walked away from her violent urges, it got worse.

The dining room table was set, and food was put out. Ryan had made pancakes, waffles, bacon, and hash browns. Two plates faced each other on the table, each plate garnished with toast already. There was a wide variety of beverages in the middle of the table as well.

"What's with the feast?" asked Abby.

Ryan smiled, pulled out a chair, and motioned Abby to sit. Abby sat. "I figured we worked up an appetite with our tournament last night. Plus, I don't know what breakfast food you like, so a little bit of everything seemed like a good choice," he joked. "I want you to know that I don't usually have women over," he said.

Abby gave him a weird look. "Okay . . .," she said, confused.

Ryan's phone began ringing. He reached in his pocket. "Yeah," he answered. She recognized the voice. It was Phil. "I have to take this," he said. Abby nodded, and he left the room, closing the balcony door behind him. It wasn't long before he came back. "Phil needs to speak with us again. It shouldn't take too long," he said.

Abby really didn't get a good feeling off Phil. "I have to work tonight," she said. *Phew!* thought Abby.

"Why don't I set something up for tomorrow morning then?" he reasoned.

"That's fine," Abby agreed. "Don't you have to work?" she asked.

"I am working today. I'll be reviewing videos of surrounding businesses to try and get a lead on the firebug case."

Abby got up and walked over to Ryan, who was now sitting at the opposite end of the table. She pulled the chair close to him and hugged him for a moment. Ryan looked at her, confused.

"Are you okay?" he asked.

Abby looked at him deeply. *Nothing,* she thought, *not an evil thought in his body.* "I want you to be careful. These streets have changed, and I don't think you realize how much just yet," she said with worry in her voice.

"That's funny," said Ryan, smirking. "I was about to say the same thing to you."

Sirens filled the streets, now more than usual. Yellow tape blocked off the area that once welcomed a large amount of foot traffic. Abby looked on with the rest of the bystanders as Liz and Ryan were loaded into ambulances, and Duffy's was gone, burned to the ground. The bodies of six men were discovered, burned beyond recognition. The reporters were already on scene and blaming the firebug of the area.

"Abby?" said a voice from the other side of the tape. It was Phil. He was getting out of the back of the ambulance that held Ryan. He motioned for the drivers to wait a moment. "What can you tell me about what happened? Were you there?" he asked as he lifted the tape and motioned for her to come over.

"Is he stable?" she said, completely dismissing Phil's question.

"It was a shoulder shot, clean through and through."

Abby was relieved. It looked so much worse when it happened. "And Liz?" she asked.

"Her injuries were much more intensive," answered Phil. "We really need a statement regarding what happened."

Abby looked at Phil with hatred. The prying he was doing was starting to make her blood boil again. Without asking permission, she got into the back of the ambulance with Ryan. The paramedic in the back closed the doors, and they went on their way. Phil looked on as they drove away. His distrust for her was already clear.

Ryan wasn't responding, even though he was stable. The IV fluid going into his arm was attached to a bag clearly marked morphine.

"He'll be comfortable for a while now, miss," said the paramedic.

She looked at him. A name tag that said "Vince" had small drops of Ryan's blood on it. Despite his job, he seemed pleasant. "My name's Abby," she said, trying to be as friendly as possible for her.

"I'm Vince." He smiled. His dark skin covered the blood that was drying on his arms. "Seems like it's going to be one of those nights again," he said, trying to make light of everything.

His eyes were bloodshot, and his face showed many signs of fatigue. Emergency workers were so overworked lately. Abby couldn't make conversation with him. There were way too many thoughts going through her mind right now. Were these guys connected to the giant freak who attacked her the previous night, or was it just another Harmon crime? Too many questions and absolutely no answers.

"We're here," the paramedic announced.

The second paramedic came around and helped unloading Ryan into the hospital. A second ambulance pulled in behind them. This one had lights and sirens going. Abby walked up to the next ambulance that carried Liz. The doors opened with haste. Liz's face had swelled on the side where her head had been cut open, and her body was so beat-up.

"Is she going to be okay?" she asked as one of the paramedics stepped down and began to unload Liz.

"We'll be taking her directly into surgery, where the doctor on call is waiting," responded the paramedic.

As they pulled the stretcher down, Liz's arm fell off the stretcher and hung limp. Abby placed her hands over her mouth while her eyes filled up with tears. After considering her options for a moment, Abby left. Going into a hospital when you're anger is melting things and igniting them isn't a safe option. She had caused enough trouble.

The walk home was a rush. It was well after curfew. The sound of police radios and K9 dogs filled the air. It was like the city of Harmon was turning into its own military state. When Abby arrived home, many of the emergency vehicles had moved on. The yellow caution tape was still in place, but a lot of it had already fallen down and was blowing in the wind. She quickly walked past Duffy's lot and approached her building. When she got into her apartment, she slammed her door behind her. She couldn't even bear to look at Ryan's door. Abby sat and looked around her small apartment. She knew the gang members were the ones who hurt Ryan and Liz but still couldn't help but blame herself. Now she had no job and no friends once again. *I can't stay here,* she thought. Was that huge freak going to show up in her apartment again? Was *she* going to hurt anymore people? Were Ryan and Liz better off without her? Too many questions without an answer. She needed answers. Abby ran to her closet and grabbed an aged leather backpack. She grabbed products from the bathroom and ran out, throwing them onto her bed. She cleaned out her dresser and packed as much as she could. After she locked the door to her apartment, she slipped the key under Ryan's door and left the building.

It was cold. The snow had fallen fast and hard while Abby was rushing around. All evidence of what happened was gone other than the rubble and ash lying where Duffy's used to be. It was odd to see. Duffy's pub had been there so long, but the midnight air made everything feel more at ease. Abby walked down a few blocks and went to the closest bank machine. On the screen, it displayed an account balance of $85.

"That's pathetic," Abby said, mocking herself.

She cleaned out her account and removed the card. A dark alley was directed across the street. Abby went down it and pulled out a knife from her boot. She cut up her debit card and then smashed her cell phone against the concrete. If she was going to find out what was going on, then no one was going to be able to follow her. The alley was getting darker and more narrow. *Who built this?* Abby thought. The end of the alley never seemed to come; instead, it was curved and continued on and on. A shadow sneaked across the stone siding. Abby ducked into an opening between two ghetto-looking buildings. It was him, that seven-foot freak who wouldn't leave her alone. *How did he find me? I didn't even know I was going to be here,* she thought. As he got closer, he began to slow down. It was as if he sensed her presence. Abby slowly bent down and grabbed her knife from her boot again. She felt so different. Instead of fear, this freak was bringing her annoyance. Instead of crying, she got angry. Instead of running, it was time to face him. She came out once he had walked slightly past her position. He stopped and turned around quickly. Finally, they were face-to-face, and Abby got to surprise him for once. The alley was dark, but she could finally see his face. It was much rounder than she remembered. His eyebrows were so thick that it looked like he only had one giant eyebrow across his forehead. His eyes drooped, and his teeth were much longer and sharper than a regular person.

"Who are you?" Abby demanded to know. He took a small step closer, straightening out his body and staring down at Abby. Abby held the knife out, ready to attack as well. "I asked who you are," Abby said sternly, attempting to stand her ground.

Instead of answering when he opened his mouth, a growling sound echoed through the alley. He reached out and grabbed Abby's throat. His hand was so large that it was able to wrap all the way around her neck with ease. Her feet slowly lifted off the ground. Abby attempted to use her knife as she thrust it into his midsection, but it wouldn't penetrate his skin. After many tries, the blade finally broke. The sound of the broken knife hitting the ground became distant as Abby blacked out.

Abby woke up on a large bed. The room was ridiculous. The bedposts looked to be made out of pure gold, and the floors were marble. This room was bigger than her whole apartment. The freak was nowhere in sight, thank God. Abby coughed as she touched her neck. She could feel the tenderness where the bruises had formed.

"Hello!" she yelled, her voice still strained from the trauma to her throat.

Nothing but silence. *How long have I been out?* she thought. Abby got up using the wall the help her keep her balance. She made her way over to a small window on the other side of the room. The window had bars on it, and when she looked out, it was facing over all of Harmon. *I must be in the Townsquare building,* she thought. But why? And why was she still alive? As Abby looked on, she began to regain her bearings. She stepped back from the window and looked around the room. She held her head, thinking about her next move. Two large double doors with those obnoxious lion door handles were at the bottom of the bed. Abby tried them.

"Of course, they're locked. That would be too easy," she said out loud.

Right as Abby was about to walk away, the door handle moved, and the door cracked open. Two women entered the room. They were small women, both with dark hair and dark tanned skin.

"Welcome home, ma'am," the two women said at once. "We're here to prepare you for your meeting," one of the women said. Their faces were completely expressionless even as she spoke.

"Meeting?" Abby asked.

"Our master will clear things up in time." The women walked over to the head of the bed and opened a chest that was directly beside it. They pulled out a gown.

"Please remove your clothes," one of the women directed. When Abby failed, the women approached her and attempted to remove her jacket.

"Don't touch me!" yelled Abby, striking one of the women in the face.

The other woman bent down to check on her colleague, and Abby made a break for the door. She closed and locked them inside. "What a couple of creeps," she said to herself. She could hear whispers, horrible whispers. She was used to hearing evil, but the amount of evil in this building was unbearable.

"You aren't a very polite dinner guest," said a deep voice.

Abby's eyes searched, but she couldn't see the person attached to the voice. The hallways were more like dark tunnels. She came to a blackened lobby with doors leading to another room. Abby tried to turn back, but the doors swung open. The room was dark except for two oddly placed torches that were lit beside a rose gold chair. Once she was inside, the doors slammed behind her. Five more torches on each side of the room lit up, allowing her to see the gaudy place completely. Gruesome art covered the walls. Statues of evil figures and terrified people filled the room.

"Okay, I'm here! You got what you wanted! Enough with the show, and let's get on with it!" Abby snapped.

The last torch lit directly behind the throne, drawing Abby's eye back up to that platform. A man was now sitting there. He had black hair with a red shine to it, pale skin, and a red hint to his eyes. *He looks like me,* Abby thought. He stared down at her without saying a word for a moment.

"Abigail Briggs, you're a very difficult woman to catch," he said with the same deep voice that already reprimanded her.

"Clearly, not hard enough," she replied sarcastically.

"Don't be so hard on yourself," he replied. "From what I know about you, if you didn't want to be caught, you wouldn't have been."

Abby took a step forward. "You know nothing about me."

"I know your mother abandoned you for any guy that would buy her cigarettes," he replied. "I know that you try connecting with people but can't because when you're with them, every dark thought comes to the surface." He continued. "And I know that you keep blocking your father out of your thoughts."

Abby turned around and walked toward the door. "Now I know you're a loon. I've never met my father."

He laughed the most evil laugh you could imagine. "I never said you did," he replied. "But if you let him speak to you, all your problems will be yesterday's news." He got up and walked down the small stairs from his over-the-top throne. "I'm Alexander. I'm your brother, and it's time for you to come home."

Alexander put his hand out as though he was expecting Abby to take it, but Abby kept pulling on the door with no luck. Defeated and fed up, she said, "You're right." She put her head against the back of the door and sighed. "You're right about me hearing the darkness in people, but I can't hear anything from you."

Alexander walked to her and put his hand on her shoulder. "That's because we're the same, and I have no ill intent."

Abby pushed his hand off her and laughed. "Maybe," she acknowledged. "Or maybe you wear your evil so close to the surface that I don't have to look deep to sense it."

Abby knocked over the torch beside her, and it filled the room quickly with fire. She grabbed the broken base of the torch and smashed the door so hard it busted open, breaking the lock. She ran out of the room, and instead of the fire staying in the room, it followed her and nipped at her feet. She gained speed and didn't stop when she came to a window at the end of her path. Her arms covered her face as her body smashed through the window. After falling for what seemed like forever, Abby landed in a deep pool that put out the fire on the flaming debris that fell with her into the pool. She got out of the pool coughing. There was no time to rest. She looked around and ran to a sewer opening that was at the back of the grounds. As she climbed inside, Alexander was joining a crowd of his men who were forming around the pool, including the giant freak who brought her there. She got in and quietly placed the top back over the manhole.

The sewer was filled with the usual fowl mess. The walls were covered in a dark slime, and she would notice the occasional rat running alongside her. Small amounts of slush from the slope on the surface made it hard for Abby to keep her footing. Her favorite thigh-high boots were being tested to their limits today. An odd feeling crept over Abby. The thought of having a brother or any kind of family was always such a comfort to Abby. Now she just wished her father's evil blood would quit plaguing the world. It was not like she could just kill herself. Suicidal thoughts had always been a burden to her. The scar on her wrist was from the first person she killed. He had grabbed her, and she watched him burn to ash. These memories never came to the surface until now. Abby recanted in her head when she tried to open her veins before, only to find out her blood clotted so fast that she couldn't bleed out. Or the time when she swallowed a whole bottle of pills, only to have her system metabolize them so quickly that they didn't affect her at all. Abby learned quickly that when you can't seem to die, you have to learn how to live.

It wasn't long before a glimpse of light shone into the tunnel from the approaching dead end. It was finally morning. When Abby got to the end of the tunnel, the light reflected off the bars from the drainage system as if they were mocking her. Without hesitation, Abby placed her hands on the two bars in the middle and began pulling with all her might. The metal began to glow, and within second, they were melted to a consistency that was able to be bent. The opening was just big enough for her to fit through now. She was almost in the clear. Abby's legs gave out, and she fell into the small river that the sewer system ran into. She pulled herself with all her might onto a small dirt shore by a rooting old pine tree. The tree had provided enough shelter that the small dusting of snow under it was nothing compared with the rest of the city. *I'm so tired,* she thought. Abby felt weak and ashamed before remembering she hadn't slept at all. That was all the justification she needed to give into what her eyes were already forcing her to do. The sound of the river faded as Abby went into a deep sleep.

Chapter 4

The sound of a crackling fireplace mixed with absolute silence was broken by a familiar voice. Abby woke in a much different state than she remembered passing out in. She was covered by an old quilt and propped up with two large plush pillows. She looked around as her eyes adjusted. She was waking up in a lot of random places lately. Her legs swung over and dropped to the floor. Small cuts from the fall Abby took out of the window were already beginning to heal. She was on an old couch next to a vintage-looking fireplace. Her jacket and boots were drying over the mantle. Low voices were chatting. It was coming from the next room. Abby noticed the door was slightly left open. As she peaked out the crack in the door, she saw Phil standing on the phone.

"Yes, Chief, we're at the safe house now," he said before he hung up and directed another person out of sight to go check on Abby. Abby closed the door and held it shut as the person on the other end tried to enter.

"Abby, it's me," said a strained voice.

"Ryan!"

She opened the door to see Ryan standing there. His arm was in a sling from the gunshot, and he had dark circles under his eyes. Ryan grabbed Abby, and the two embraced.

"I've been looking everywhere for you." He hugged her so tight it made up for him only being able to use one arm.

"How did I get here?" she asked.

"A patrol vehicle spotted you, and when Phil heard your description over the radio, he picked me up, and we came straight to get you."

Abby continued holding onto Ryan. "I'm so glad you're okay, and Liz?" Abby asked.

Ryan looked at Abby with an alarming look as he gently shook his head. "I'm afraid she had internal bleeding that couldn't be stopped." Abby hung her head and bit her lip, trying everything she could to prevent herself from tearing up. Ryan continued. "What happened? Did they hurt you?"

"No," she went on. "But this time he was able to take me."

Ryan came in the room and sat on the couch Abby woke up on. "Where did he take you?" Ryan quickly asked.

"He took me to see a man named Alexander."

Ryan's face seemed to go completely white, almost whiter than her. His lips trembled as he asked, "I need to know where he is."

Abby looked away from him and softly said, "I can't tell you." With his face now turning into rage, Abby tried to explain, "If I tell you, you're going to go there. And you're going to die."

Ryan stood and paced the length of the room. "You need to tell me where he is now, Abby, for the girls."

Abby paused in thought and looked at Ryan. "What girls?" she asked.

"Shortly after I was put onto the firebug case, two young girls went missing. We worked day and night on both cases but ended up finding their bodies. The only link between them was that they were last seen talking to Alexander's men."

Abby looked into the fire. "But that's not really why you want to find him, is it?"

Ryan's face was once again overcome with pale terror as the anger was flushed out. "No," he said, sitting back beside her. As they looked into the fire together, Ryan sighed deeply. "Alexander was the one who killed my family," he confessed.

Abby had already figured that out but gave him a moment before moving closer to him. "I'm sorry," she said.

Ryan looked at her, confused. "You haven't done anything wrong. Why would you be sorry?"

Abby looked away from Ryan again and back to the fire. "Because I was so close to him," she said with anger in her voice. "I was so close, and I didn't kill him."

Abby and Ryan emerged from the back room. "There's coffee," Phil said roughly.

Ryan walked in behind Phil toward the coffee. "He gets moody when he's tired," Ryan said, smiling at Abby.

Phil was sitting alone at a dining room table. Another fireplace was lit in the joining sitting room. The fire danced across the walls, bringing them to life. Phil's gun was sitting on the table in front of him. He was prepared for anything that came through that door. Abby considered the possibility that she may have misjudged Phil's character. Either way, she had bigger problems. From what she had gathered, her father was the most evil being ever to exist, and her half brother was trying to live like him here in Harmon. The worst part was that the one person Abby wanted to confide in and tell all this to was the one person she couldn't. Ryan was used to chasing men with guns. The type of evil he'd seen was nothing compared with what would be waiting for him inside that building. The presence of fire calmed Abby, but torches lighting by themselves surrounding a throne was the type of evil layer trickery that would throw any mortal cop off their game, no matter how good of an officer they were. It seemed like Ryan and the rest of the police force were starting a manhunt for Alexander. But how could she tell them that he was not merely a man?

As Ryan poured coffee into two plain white mugs, Abby sat next to Phil. His eyes were focused on a file he was leaning over. The name on the file read "Alexander Smith."

"Smith?" Abby blurted out.

Phil snapped the file shut, and instead of looking at her, he seemed to look through her. "It's classified," he stated.

Ryan laughed and sat on the other side of Phil. "His last name is unknown," he said to clear the confusion.

Abby sat quietly and sipped at her coffee. "I'll take you there, but I'm not telling you where."

Ryan looked at Abby with amazement. "Why would you ever want to go back there?"

Abby stood and took her mug over to the sink. She set it down and placed her hands on the counter. "Because I ran. I ran, and I'm tired of running."

Phil sternly stepped in. "We can't have a civilian tagging along."

Abby picked her mug and smashed it against the wall. "A civilian! A fucking civilian! You wouldn't even know he was here if it weren't for me!"

Phil placed his hand on his gun, and Abby's eyes narrowed as she stared in his face. The fire in the sitting room exploded into a large inferno. Ryan's focus quickly turned to fighting the fire. As he struggled with his injured arm to control the fire extinguisher, Phil ran to him and took control. Ryan looked at Abby as tears filled her eyes. She ran to the room she woke up in, locked the door, and began putting on her boots. Ryan busted in within moments after the fire was contained to find an empty room. He saw that Abby and all her belongings were gone. She had quickly slipped out the window and already disappeared out of sight.

The anger and rage inside were building up to a breaking point. Now instead of forgetting the crazy things happening while Abby was blacked out, she remembers all of it. How could she help Ryan at the pub fire but almost kill him at the safe house? All Abby knew for certain right now was that she needed to get as far away from the people she cared about as possible. The thought of Liz dying alone in a hospital bed played tricks on Abby's mind as she walked through the cold night air. She couldn't help but condemn herself for not going to the hospital with Liz. As she walked through the night, distant whispers took on the tone of Liz's voice as though Abby's mind refused to believe her death was real and was trying to keep her alive. The cemetery in Harmon had grown a lot over the past twenty years. It was once contained in a small churchyard. Now it was the size of many city blocks. Walking through a cemetery might be eerie for some, but for Abby, it was calming. It's the only place where you can walk through a crowd and not a single person has one evil thought or an ounce of ill intention. Sometimes the living can be exhausting.

At the edge of the cemetery under a huge old pine tree was a freshly dug grave. As much as Abby wanted to walk the other way, her legs seemed to have their own plans. The snow was beginning to melt away from the sun of the day, making the ground muddy and unsteady. As Abby neared the grave, a pine cone fell and sunk into the freshly dug earth at the foot of the headstone. Abby read the stone and fell to her knees. Mud splashed up her face and soaked into her pants. It said, "Elizabeth Duffy." It was Liz. It was true, and this time there was no holding back the tears.

"I'm so sorry, Liz. I'm so sorry," Abby cried. She was so distracted she didn't even notice the man approaching from behind. A soft hand touched her shoulder, and without looking up, Abby's voice cracked as she asked, "Why did you follow me?"

Ryan helped her to her feet and spun her around. "Because you were right. Without you, we wouldn't have any leads, and we would be aimlessly searching for Alexander for another twenty years," Ryan explained. "And if you think I'm letting you wander off alone, you're even more nuts than what happened back there."

Abby looked at Ryan, waiting for him to ask the impossible question that was inevitable, but instead, he took her by the hand and started walking toward his car.

"I don't know how it happens or how to stop it," she said out of the blue.

Ryan still looked shaken from the events over the last few days, but if he was upset with Abby, he never once let on. "I guess that's something we can figure out together. Phil is convinced something else got into the fireplace and caused what happened."

Abby looked around. "Where is he?" she asked.

"He's heading back to the station to fill the chief in on the events," Ryan answered. As they got to the car, Ryan stepped in front of Abby quickly and opened the passenger door. Abby sat, and Ryan closed it. He sprinted around to the driver's side. The keys were still in the ignition. Ryan turned to Abby and said, "Maybe we should just keep some of the details between us for now."

Abby smiled, and her body began to relax. Ryan started the car and began to drive. "Where are we headed?" she asked.

"There's another safe house outside the city. This time I think it might be best if only the two of us know our location."

Abby put her hand on Ryan's thigh. She wasn't sure why he was so understanding or why he cared about her, but she accepted it. She needed it. "Thank you," she said. "Thank you for trying to understand something that makes absolutely no sense."

Ryan smiled and placed his hand in hers while they continued driving in silence, though it was obvious both their minds were racing.

Chapter 5

"We're here," Ryan said softly as he gently pushed the hair out of Abby's eyes.

Abby looked around. She must have dozed off on the drive. They had driven down a long driveway to an old country-style home. It looked completely abandoned. Boards were covering the windows, making it look even less appealing than it already was.

"Sorry," Abby said, "I didn't mean to doze off."

Ryan got out of the car and went around to Abby's side. He opened the door and guided her out. "We'll get a few hours of sleep. Then we'll figure out where to go from here," he said.

Abby followed Ryan up the old porch to a dirty wooden door. She noticed grass was growing into the porch. No one had lived there for a long time. Ryan entered first, motioning for Abby to follow. The outside of the house gave a false impression of what the inside would look like. Other than a large layer of dust of everything, it had a very relaxed country feel. The best part was there was no fireplace. Abby took her jacket off and flung it over an old saddle that was hanging on the left side of the wall. To the right was the kitchen. Ryan was already in there, finding supplies for the evening. Abby walked to the back of the home, where there were multiple doors, one leading to the bathroom, which she utilized first. After all, it was a long trip. It was very small and only had a tub with no shower. Once she finished in the bathroom, she continued exploring. The door directly across from the bathroom led to a small bedroom, although it was probably considered large way back when the house was built. There was a double bed in the middle of the room. The headboard had the design of horses running and looked so majestic. The comforter was green with floral decor on it. It wasn't the best by any means, but if she had the option to stay here with Ryan forever, she would take it.

Back in the kitchen, Ryan had hit pay dirt, finding two large cans of beans and molasses. Gross, sure, but after not eating for a couple of days, anything was better than passing out. He emptied them into a large pot. Abby walked in as he was attempting to light the aged gas stove. He was swearing and losing his cool. Abby looked at the stove for a second, and it ignited. The beans started boiling.

"Got it!" yelled Ryan.

Abby smiled. "You sure did."

They sat together with two bowls and began talking. Abby had never been so open with anyone in her life. They shared stories about their childhood and horror stories about foster homes, and Ryan shared memories of his parents.

"So you've never met your dad?" asked Ryan.

"No, I mean . . . he tries to speak to me, but I block him out," Abby tried explaining.

Ryan was puzzled. "Not a good influence then?" he asked.

Abby laughed. "You have no idea." Abby got up after noticing they had both stopped eating and took their bowls to the sink. Ryan turned in his chair to continue facing Abby.

"Why do you avoid talking about your family?" he asked.

Abby paused. "Trying to explain things has always made me sound insane, so I just don't anymore."

Ryan got up and joined Abby by the sink. "I hope there's a time in the future where you'll tell me." His hand stroked Abby's hair.

Abby smiled. *Only if I want to lose you fast,* she thought. "I'm going to go clean myself up if that's okay," Abby said, turning around from the sink.

"Of course," Ryan said as his eyes followed her down the hall.

The water pressure was terrible in this little cabin. It was the quickest bath Abby had ever had. Abby was shivering when she turned around to realize she forgot to check for towels before she even got in the tub. Her clothing was still wet and dirty, and this tiny shack had no heat in winter. She ran across the hall into the bedroom. To her surprise, Ryan was already in the bed. He had washed off in the sink while she was in the bathroom. She stood there for a moment, thinking about what to do. As her breath got deeper, she noticed it was visible in the cold air. Freezing, she got under the covers with him. He rolled over and faced her. Her hair was still damp and drying in a nice beach wave. Her skin wasn't red anymore. It was back to her natural pale look but covered in goose bumps as she shivered, clutching the blanket.

Ryan wrapped himself around Abby's naked body. She could feel his flesh, indicating he was completely nude also. She was so tired and so upset over the past couple of days, yet she still wanted him. Her shivering stopped as Ryan's warmth radiated into her body. Abby felt an overwhelming sense of calm, something she had only felt with Ryan. They looked deep into each other's eyes and began kissing passionately. Ryan's lips moved from her lips to her cheek and then down by her neck. It was so intense it was as though two foster kids had finally found a home within each other.

His mouth stopped at her ear and whispered to her, "I don't want to pressure you with all that's happening."

He may be a gentleman, but his body didn't wait for her to answer. She could feel his erection pressed against her leg. Abby wrapped her legs around Ryan.

"With everything that's happening, we might not get another chance," she said to him.

She could feel him, swollen and ready. It wasn't his body that was holding back. He definitely had a strong mind. Abby pushed him off her. He fell down on the bed on his back. She playfully climbed on top of him, teasing him by lowering herself on top of him. Ryan grabbed Abby's hips and forced her down on him hard, impaling her with his whole length. Abby yelled out in pleasure. She was so excited. Ryan could feel her juices dripping down his shaft. Ryan put his arms around Abby and pulled her into him more. Her boobs bounced on his face. The excitement was too much. Ryan flipped her over, pulling her ass in the air. Abby's cries of pleasure were muffled by the pillow that her face was forced into while Ryan filled her from behind. A final thrust sent sensations surging through both their bodies as they reached climax together and fell side by side once again.

They lay awake for hours, facing each other and talking. Abby even talked about the future, something she never thought she even had. It was both exciting and tragic. Abby finally wanted to live and wanted a future at a time where no one's future was certain.

Ryan was starting to fade into a deep sleep as he moaned, "I love you."

That was the first time anyone had ever said that to Abby before except for a stuffed dog she bought herself for Valentine's Day a few years back. She wasn't sure how to reply. She was afraid she would tear up, so she rolled over and looked away. Ryan moved closer to her and wrapped his arms around her. At least he wasn't just expecting her to say it back. Ryan's whole body was touching her. Spooning, that was something else she'd never done before. She wasn't a prude by any means. Abby had sexual partners before, but she had never even had an orgasm before. Ryan was opening her up to new emotions and experiences that she didn't know were possible. The negative had always ruled her life before him.

Abby woke up blinded. Ryan had removed one of the boards last night on the bedroom window, and the sun was beaming in. Ryan rolled over.

"Good morning," he said with a smile. He leaned in and gave Abby a soft kiss.

"Good morning," she replied.

His eyes still had small crusts in the corner from sleeping. His hair was messed up just enough to make Abby's heart skip a beat. She'd never had someone to wake up to before. It was actually a great feeling. Ryan's phone was flashing.

"Nineteen missed calls," he read out loud. Abby grabbed his phone and quickly got out of bed. She wrapped Ryan's sweater around her as she opened the back of the phone. "What are you doing?" asked Ryan.

"No, what are you doing? You said our location would be between us. They could track us with this," Abby said in a fright.

Ryan got up out of the bed slowly. "Calm down," he said as he slowly took the phone out of her hands. "It's a burner phone. No one's tracking us with this."

Abby sighed. "I'm sorry, I just don't want them finding us."

Ryan pulled his jeans on and sat on the bed. "The man that was in your apartment before?" Ryan asked but already knew the answer.

"Yes," she replied.

"Was it Alexander?" he asked.

"No," she replied, trying to be as vague as possible, "but he works for him."

Abby sat beside Ryan. It was time to explain things even if it meant losing him because losing him wouldn't be as hard as watching him die. It was obvious he was going to keep looking for him with or without her.

"Alexander isn't like the other criminals you've put away," she stated.

Ryan's annoyance was unable to be hidden. "You've already said that," he said.

Abby could see beating around the bush wasn't going to work this time. "He's like a devil!" she shouted.

Ryan's face changed from being annoyed to showing sheer confusion. Confusion was better than the disbelief Abby expected. "What do you mean? He's evil?" asked Ryan.

"Yes, among other things," Abby explained. "Have you ever seen him before?" she asked.

Ryan shook his head in disappointment. "I've gotten so close before, but he's always one step ahead of me."

Abby automatically knew why. If he was so much like her, then he could hear Ryan's ill intent toward him from miles away. No wonder he was always ahead of them.

"You'll never catch up to him on your own," Abby said.

This was the first time Ryan ever looked angry at her. "So you expect me just to give up? He killed my family, Abby! He's abducted multiple girls! He's a monster!"

Abby liked the hatred Ryan had toward Alexander. "His men killed Liz," she added.

Ryan's breathing softened as did his face. "Is that true?" he asked.

"They were wearing his colors, black and red, the same colors the men at his hideout were wearing. They killed Liz," Abby repeated.

Ryan placed his hand on Abby's leg. "Then how can you expect me to walk away from this?" he asked.

Abby looked Ryan directly in the eyes. "I never said to walk away. I said you can't do it on your own."

Ryan smiled. "I can't ask you to do this."

Abby got up and started getting dressed. "You didn't ask. I go with or without you. But I would prefer staying with you."

"You want to stay with me?" Ryan asked.

"Yes," said Abby.

That was all he needed to hear. Ryan got up and began loading his gun. Abby got her answer.

They didn't get back into the city until after curfew, which worked out great for them. The only people on the streets were other officers whom Ryan knew or criminals, which was exactly what they were looking for. The snow was finally melted away. Ryan parked the car on a dead-end side street, and they left on foot as not to be noticeable. Ryan held onto Abby's hand so tight. She wasn't sure if it was out of fear for her safety or just out of fear in general. She didn't care, though, as long as he didn't let go. They came up to a checkpoint. A large officer approached them. He had dark skin, black hair, and a small scar above his lip. He smiled at Abby before looking to Ryan.

"Work permits, sir?"

Ryan pulled out his badge. The uniformed officer took it and began reading the badge number over the radio. The volume was down, just low enough so Abby couldn't make out what was being said. He stood there a moment with the radio up to his ear, waiting for a reply.

"Sorry about that, sir. You're all clear." He handed Ryan's badge back and shook his hand.

They continued walking as Abby jokingly asked, "Sir?"

Ryan laughed and explained how detectives were a bit higher on the chain of command than uniformed officers. He acted as though it was common knowledge. Maybe so but not to someone who had never talked to an officer of any kind before.

When they got to Townsquare, Abby's heart began to race, and she stopped.

"If you can't do this, I can get Phil to pick you up," Ryan offered.

"Don't even think about calling him!" she snapped. She couldn't bring herself to trust him, and usually, there were good reasons.

Abby walked ahead fast, making a point that she was ready and willing. The tall Townsquare building was dark but different this time. She walked around the back of the building.

"He's not here anymore," she said.

"How can you tell?" Ryan asked as he followed her.

"Because he's always with his men, and they aren't here," she said.

"I'm still confused," Ryan said.

Glass crunched under Abby's boot. She looked up to see the window she willingly jumped from. The glass was still shining at the bottom of the pool while they walked past.

"What the hell happened here?" Ryan said with a look of shock on his face.

Abby stopped and turned to Ryan with a smirk. "Well, I had to get out someway," she said as she walked toward the building.

Ryan looked up at the window and down at the pool. It must have been at least ten stories high. His amazement that she was able to survive a jump like that was overshadowed by the wonder of what kind of evil could make someone choose smashing through a window to their potential death. His thought was interrupted by the loud unoiled hinges on the old doors as Abby took it upon herself to enter.

"Wait up!" Ryan said, having his gun ready with his good arm.

Everything was gone, even the drywall. It looked like the whole place had been burned, but it mysteriously went out after the drywall burned up. The fire damage didn't seem to go near the structure of the building at all. It was dark and damp. They got to a dark open area with two large doors on the other end.

"That's where Alexander was," she said, remembering.

She swung the doors open before Ryan could stop her to come up with a plan. It wouldn't have mattered because nothing was there anyway. The art that was covering the walls had burned, along with the rest of the decor. The throne he sat on was gone as were all the torches.

"Can you show me where they held you?" Ryan asked.

Abby nodded. "Back out this way," she said.

She closed her eyes and tried to remember how to navigate the halls in the big old building. The last time she was so distracted, the men in that building had such evil minds that it overwhelmed her. Abby was able to find her way back this time. It was so much easier with just Ryan. Instead of clouding her mind, he gave her so much clarity.

Ryan pushed his way in front of Abby and entered the room first, his gun drawn. Ryan's gun dropped as Abby entered, his eyes focused on the bed. Lying there was a young girl, maybe fourteen at most. Her eyes were hazed over, all life drained out of them. Her stomach was opened up, her organs removed. It was the missing girl Ryan had a picture of. She must have been in the same building while Abby was held.

"I have to call this in," Ryan said.

"Wait," said Abby.

She walked over and placed her hand on the girl's forehead. She was cold and had definitely been dead for quite a few hours. Abby's hand glowed. Ryan's grandfather was a welder before he passed away. Luckily for him, it was well before Harmon went to hell. The metal a welder would heat would glow similar to what was happening to Abby when it was heated. The girl's final thoughts weren't evil but were filled with terror. Abby saw the giant freak picking her and throwing her by the neck, paralyzing her. Alexander removed anything he could use for his own needs from her body. As he sliced into her, she felt everything. She was awake. She wanted to go home. Abby took her hand off her and began sobbing.

"He tortured her," she cried. "He tortured her, and she just wanted to go home."

Ryan couldn't understand, but he did understand that his confusion was becoming the norm. Ryan called it in anonymously so they could continue without questions. Ryan and Abby left Townsquare and got back to the car. His lights had already been smashed by someone who was fleeing on foot. They got in the car and locked the doors, ignoring the vandal. Ryan pulled Abby into him and held her tightly.

"I don't know how you escaped, but I'm so glad you did," he whispered to her.

She rested her head on his chest while they sat in silence for a while. The girl's milky dead eyes were burned into Abby's mind. So many thoughts crowded her head. If her father was so evil and her brother was insanely bad, then wasn't she evil? If she was evil, then why would a random girl's death bother her? Would Ryan still love her if it turned out the fires she had caused were connected to his firebug case? Abby's head began to ache. As strong as they both were, this wasn't a scene they wanted to remember.

Chapter 6

A tall glass slammed down on a rundown bar counter. Ryan sat across from Abby at the table she had grabbed for them. A few drinks after that experience was definitely needed. The bar was filled with people of all ages. Ryan's badge was hidden as he sat. People breaking curfew wasn't something he held in high priority at the current point in time. As they began to sip on their drinks and try to rid their minds of the gruesome images they encountered, the people in the bar began to run toward the doors. It was a curfew sweep. The officers were decked out in riot gear and grabbed the patrons as they ran out of the bar in their drunken hazes. The bar was pretty much empty now except for Abby and Ryan. The main doors flung open, and Phil emerged from the streets.

"When you said you had to take care of something, I didn't think you would disappear for days," Phil said, looking toward Ryan.

"A lot has happened. We just needed to catch our breath," explained Ryan.

"You can do that down at the station!" snapped Phil.

He grabbed Ryan by the arm that wasn't in a sling and whispered to another officer while walking Ryan to his car. A female officer came and grabbed Abby. Abby noticed the grip the female officer had on her arm was much more aggressive than just a simple assisting touch. When she got outside, she made eye contact with Ryan, who was already in the back of the car. Phil was in the front seat and looked to be talking to him. Abby looked at Phil's lips, and even though she obviously couldn't hear anything, she could hear gentle whispers, whispers that turned her stomach. The things Phil were thinking about doing were unspeakable. She never liked him and knew something was up, but he was evil, but this was the first time the whispers were crystal clear.

"Why are we taking separate cars?" Abby asked the cop leading her.

"Sit down," demanded the cop. She stood pointing at the open car door.

Abby sat in the car while continuing to look back at Phil and Ryan.

After many attempts to talk to the bitch in the front seat, Abby gave up. After a few moments, the female officer asked Abby's full name and age. No one seemed to want to address Abby anyway, so she declined to answer any further questions. A few minutes had gone by when Abby turned her head to look back. Phil and Ryan were nowhere to be seen. They had been driving behind them for blocks.

"Where's the other car?" asked Abby.

The other cop didn't answer, but Abby saw her roll her eyes in the rearview mirror. The cop looked up for a moment, and confusion swept over her face. She picked up the radio and called to Phil.

"Detective Deeks, please respond." She continued.

"What's going on? Where are they?" Abby was panicking.

"They probably took a shortcut. We'll meet them at the station," said the useless officer.

Abby could feel that something was wrong. She closed her eyes and focused on Phil's face, the moment she looked at his lips and heard his evil thoughts. Perhaps she could recreate the events in her head without having to be standing right in front of him. She focused on him, the angered look always in his eyes, the same cold dead eyes she had seen before. Abby's mind went blank as she only focused on him. Then the flash of an image appeared. Abby saw a shovel with a mixture of blood and dirt on it. She saw Phil's eyes go even colder than she could have imagined. She was seeing Ryan's death.

"You have to go back and find them!" she screamed. "Maybe it hasn't happened yet!"

The officer in the front rightfully had no idea what Abby was talking about. "Sit down and shut up!" she shouted at Abby. Abby leaned back as far as she could, and with all the power of her legs, she kicked out the back window. "What the fuck!" yelled the officer.

Another kick from Abby's powerful legs was all it took to knock out the back window. Before the officer could even stop the car, Abby had rolled out of her sight.

Abby had no idea where to start, but something told her it wasn't far. Just like Alexander, Phil was probably hiding right under her nose. Abby could hear Ryan's screams, but it seemed like no one else could. She walked past a group of hooded youths spray-painting obscenities on the walkway. They got startled but continued committing their small crime once they realized Abby didn't notice or care. As Ryan's screams got louder, Abby picked up pace, running into the unknown. Abby made her way to a darkened alley with a wooden door directly across from her. As soon as she approached the door, the screams stopped. It seemed like she was heading in the right direction. Abby touched the door handle, and a ray of emotions took over her. She could see Ryan being dragged inside by Phil. He was thrown into the far corner of the building, and Phil kicked his bullet wound repeatedly. Abby couldn't explain or understand how she was able to do these things, but she didn't care at the moment as long as they worked in Ryan's favor right now. Abby turned the handle, and the door creaked. She adjusted the speed to prevent further noise. Her eyes peered in to see the situation she chose to put herself in. She could see Ryan lying there, limp and injured. He was lying in the same position Liz was in. *I can't lose him too,* she thought. She left the door open behind her and ran toward the corner. Ryan was still there, thank God. He was barely conscious.

Abby grabbed both sides of his face and spoke softly. "Where is he?" she asked.

Ryan looked up at her. "Run, go," he said as he coughed up a small amount of blood.

Abby got chills. In her mind, she saw something else. The shovel was meant for her now. She turned around to see Phil in mid swing. Phil's face overflowed with surprise when Abby caught the shovel before striking her. Ryan tried to reach for his gun with his good arm, but Phil had already disarmed him. Abby got the shovel away from Phil right before he took out his gun. She swung the shovel at the gun, severing Phil's right hand at the wrist. Ryan yelled almost as loud as Phil. Phil fell to the floor holding his forearm and then frantically crawled around, trying to locate his hand. Blood poured and squirted as he flopped around in agony. Abby knew this was their chance to get the hell out of there. She put Ryan's good arm around her and dragged him out. He bent down on the way and grabbed his gun that Phil had thrown out of his reach. Ryan's legs tried to assist as much as he could, but Abby could tell that he was very injured.

"We can't go to the hospital," she said. "We should find a place to lie low. I'll watch you tonight," Abby said.

Ryan put his hand in hers and assured her, "I'll be fine. I just need to rest. He was my partner . . .," he said before fading away again.

Abby had carried Ryan for nearly three blocks before coming across a silver minivan parked at the side of the road. It was unlocked but didn't have keys. Luckily for Abby, her morals had been lacking most of her life, and she had learned to hot-wire a car before the age of twelve. Stealing a car seemed pretty light to Abby after cutting off a cop's hand. She took out the extra sets of seats in the back and threw them onto the sidewalk. She carefully put Ryan down in the back of the van and covered him with an old blanket that was covering one of the discarded seats. It wasn't long before the van was started, and they were on their way. Abby just wasn't sure where they were going. She tried to think of a place where they would be safe, where she wouldn't have to look over her shoulder every moment.

Nowhere. That was nowhere safe. It was obvious Alexander had cops on his payroll too. There was no one to trust. Ryan couldn't even trust his own partner. *Well, if there's nowhere safe to go,* she thought, *then that's exactly where I'll go.*

She drove out of the city and through a large wooded area. There was a small opening in between some old trees. Abby drove in between them and turned off the van and all the lights. She locked the doors and climbed in the back with Ryan. It was pretty spacious back there. With all the insults people throw at minivans, it was shocking to see just how convenient they can be in an emergency. Abby checked on Ryan.

"I'm fine," he mumbled as she touched his wrist to check his pulse.

She looked out the windows. There was absolutely nothing but trees and darkness. They were finally nowhere. Abby crawled under the blanket with Ryan after checking the locks one more time. She put her arm over him and drifted off. Sleep had never been more rare than it was lately, and she really needed her mind clear more than ever.

The sun glared into the van windows.

"Too bright," said Abby. She woke up to feel Ryan spooning her from behind. "How are you feeling?" she asked.

No answer. Unlike most people, Abby was used to very little sleep. Ryan hadn't slept in days and was a difficult case to wake up. He may have been injured, but that wasn't stopping his body from doing what every other man's body does in the morning. As she felt him pressed against her, she knew exactly how to wake him, which was a proven, foolproof method for any man. She slowly slipped under the blanket. She unzipped his jeans and reached inside his pants. He was totally out and exposed now. As her lips pressed over the tip, she massaged and tickled his length with her tongue. Her hands massaged the surrounding flesh. It was working. He was definitely waking up. His hips were now moving and grinding involuntarily. She felt his hand touch her head as he moaned and filled her mouth. She licked up every drop and sucked one last time, causing him to moan and twitch.

"Oh my god," he groaned as she emerged from under the blanket.

"Glad you're up," she said with a smirk.

"I've never had that in the morning," he said as he pulled himself to a sitting position.

Abby sat beside him. "Just trying to lighten the mood," Abby joked.

"We should probably get moving," Ryan said. "We're probably wanted by now."

Abby nodded and climbed into the driver's seat. Ryan pulled himself into the passenger seat.

"You know how to hot-wire a car?" he asked.

"I think the answer to that question is obvious," said Abby as she used the two exposed wires to start the engine.

With the beating Phil had given Ryan, Abby was just happy he woke up at all. After everything that had happened in the last few days, she felt awful for smiling but couldn't help but give in.

"Abby, I'm going to be honest with you. I have no plan. And now I have no partner. I don't even know what side of the law is the right one anymore," Ryan confessed.

"You have a partner, and we have a plan." Abby pulled the neck of her jacket down to reveal the fast-fading bruises from when the giant freak had grabbed her. "I'm bait," she said.

After driving aimlessly for some time, Abby and Ryan agreed to head back into Harmon. It was a reluctant decision. Part of them just wanted to keep driving and start a life as far away from Harmon as possible. But when you always run, it means you'll always be chased. There's nothing restful about that. As they got into the city, they noticed that the streets were bare and most stores and shops were closed, even though it was during business hours.

"It looks like everyone's afraid to leave their homes now," Ryan said as he stared out the window at the worsened state of his city.

"They won't be safe in there much longer either if something doesn't change," Abby added.

As they drove past their apartment building, they noticed a police presence staking it out. Ryan was right. They were already wanted, even though they were the ones trying to prevent these awful things from happening. Townsquare was totally blocked off. Not even foot traffic was allowed near it. They would have to go somewhere predictable enough for Alexander but not predictable enough for the Harmon police force. Abby could tell that Ryan was lost. He wanted to call in for backup or reach out, but he was too smart to blow their cover. Then she saw it, the first evil thought that had crossed Ryan's mind. He didn't want to arrest Alexander; he wanted to kill him. Ryan's head wandered, unaware that a guest was sifting through his personal thoughts. He tried rationalizing it to himself each time he thought about the murder. He knew that just because Alexander was evil, it didn't give him the right to take his life. Abby wanted to chime in, but he still didn't understand her fully. But he had seen a lot of what she could do. Perhaps he just didn't want to pry. As Abby's mind started to wander, she got further away from his mind.

"I want to kill him," she said out loud.

Ryan took her hand as she pulled over to the side of the road after feeling herself fill with violent anger again. "When we find him, whatever happens, we leave together," said Ryan.

Abby could tell that he was relieved not to be the only one with these homicidal urges toward Alexander.

Abby continued driving within the city. The tinted windows in the van she skillfully acquired provided them with much-needed privacy. It wasn't long before Ryan's words faded, and he was asleep. She occasionally nudged him to make sure he was okay. He wasn't losing any more blood, but Abby was worried about a head injury. Sure, she saw a lot of the attack but not all of it. And Ryan was pretty beat-up after Phil got done with him. Although in the grand scheme of things, cuts and bruises weren't anything compared with a severed hand. Phil definitely got the worst end of the deal in that fight.

As Abby's thoughts wandered while Ryan slept, she wondered about Phil, why he did what he did. *Was it just the money Alexander offered?* she thought. There must have been another reason for someone to turn on their partner like that. *I wonder if he even lived after that,* she thought. The last she saw was Phil flopping around like a fish holding his bloody limb. She much had happened within the last few days. Abby thought back to the beginning of the week. Her only concern was staying inside, away from people. Now she was traveling with a guy, dare she say boyfriend, and they were in a life-and-death situation. The only person she had in her life a week ago was dead, her place of employment was burned down, and apparently, she had an insanely evil brother. *Oh, and I'm wanted,* she added as if she was arguing with her own thoughts.

A blacked-out van had been keeping its distance for about four blocks now. Abby noticed it would maintain the same speed of them and occasionally slow down, but it never left the rearview mirror. She took a right down a narrow road within the industrial area of Harmon. The van followed her. Abby looked over at Ryan still sleeping, worried about what was to come. The whispers came back to her again. Ever since Liz's death, they were becoming more clear. Maybe she could use this to her benefit. She reached over and shook Ryan awake.

"We've got company," she said. He opened in eyes as much as he could and looked around. "Behind us." Abby pointed.

As Abby slowed the van to a stop, the vehicle behind them did the same, stopping only a few feet from them. Ryan took out his gun. This time his hands were shaking. It was obvious that the things he had been through lately had caught up to his body and maybe even his mind at this point. He needed his partner, but that was no longer Phil. It was now the only person he could trust and count on to have his back. Abby put her hand on his and motioned for him to put his gun away.

"I have to tell you something," she said.

"I don't think now is the time," said Ryan frantically as he looked behind the car one more time to check if they were still there.

Abby grabbed both sides of his face and turned him to directly face her. "No, now is the time," she said, looking into his eyes. "I'm so sorry that I didn't tell you sooner," she said.

"What are you talking about?" Ryan asked, still trying to look back at the suspicious vehicle behind them.

"He might be my brother," Abby admitted.

Ryan looked confused. "Who? The people following us?" he replied.

"No, Alexander. He said something about our father, but I don't know exactly," Abby explained. "I wanted to tell you sooner, but it's just been so crazy." Silence swept over the van.

"I trusted you. What else aren't you telling me?" Ryan asked in a tone that Abby hadn't heard before from him.

"Nothing. Well, there's a couple things. But they change nothing, and I'm not even sure I know how to explain them."

Ryan looked angry. "Try!" he snapped.

Abby unlocked the van doors and cracked her door open slightly, causing the interior light to go on in the van. Ryan ducked and looked behind them after realizing they were now exposed.

"This isn't explaining things!" Ryan shouted in a whispered tone. "This is suicide! They're still there!" He continued. Abby got out of the car as the blacked-out vehicle made a noise to indicate they also unlocked their doors. Ryan opened his door, unaware of the events that were about to take place. "Abby, get back in the van!" he screamed.

There was no whisper in his voice this time. Four masked men emerged from the van and stood before Abby. She could hear what they wanted to do to her. She even knew where they wanted to bury Ryan. *That's a bit much,* she thought. The largest man directed another to get Ryan out of the car. He had a very deep voice that made Abby's stomach uneasy. As the other man walked over, Ryan yelped as something pulled him back into his seat. The passenger door slammed and locked by itself. A barrier of flames about four feet tall surrounded the van, preventing anyone from going near Ryan. Their efforts turned to Abby. Ryan watched on as Abby changed, both physically and something inside her too. Abby gave his mind love and his body pleasure, but now he was seeing the side she wanted to keep from him. The evil side she feared would one day come out if she kept ignoring the violent urges within her. It was a scene much like in the pub; however, Ryan was actually conscious and watching this time. She didn't want Ryan to see this. She didn't even know what *this* was, but if she didn't do something, then there wouldn't be a Ryan left to lose anyway.

Abby's pupils dilated. Her skin glowed a remarkable pinkish-red color, and this time her long red hair flamed on the ends. Abby had no idea this would happen, but it was time to test her limits. The men's heads were filled with horribly evil images, but Abby saw it as a step-by-step guide to their actions. It was amazing. She saw what they wanted to do before they did it. The largest man came toward Abby. Before he could grab her, she had her hands around his throat. Steam was pouring out of his neck as he screamed. Abby picked him off his feet. Her eyes now turning red, the other three men ran back to their vehicle. She threw him into the side of the building with such force that the whole building began to crack and split. Flame engulfed the building. They were now surrounded by fire, the one thing Abby could control in her life. They were fucked.

Abby stared at the van. The smell of gasoline became so strong that even Ryan was gagging inside the van. The line of fire that was protecting the van holding Ryan was now spreading in a direct line to their vehicle. It was seconds before the blacked-out van was now just a pile of fire. The flames went as high as the two-story building the first guy's body destroyed. The screams of the men could be heard as they struggled to open the doors that had locked behind them when they cowardly ran off. The screams faded as the fire lessened to reveal unrecognizable and badly parched bodies. Abby's appearance went back to normal, but there was a permanent change in her mind. She spent her whole life wondering who she was, and now she didn't even know *what* she was.

The flames surrounding the van fizzled down. Abby walked around to the driver's side and got back in. She started it up and began to drive without a word. Ryan was breathing heavily and still lying back in the seat where he was thrown with force. As they pulled away from the horrific scene, Abby looked in the rearview mirror as the building continued to burn behind them. Abby was exhausted, and Ryan was in shock, or something. Abby pulled back out on the main road, finally able to see properly being away from the smoke. The sirens that were heard in the distance began getting louder.

Abby pulled into a small truck stop an intersection over. At least they were away from the bodies. Fire trucks sped past them as they parked facing the road. Ryan hadn't put his gun away yet. Instead, he had been sitting there holding it on his lap like a child with a security blanket. *Maybe I went too far this time,* Abby thought. She didn't feel like they were going to survive that encounter any other way.

Abby looked at Ryan for a moment. "Do you want to talk?" she asked.

Ryan continued to look straight ahead. His face was filled with so many emotions, mostly shock. "Who are you?" he asked.

The most vague question he could ask but so valid right now. If only Abby had an answer for him or for her. "I don't know. That's why I need to find Alexander again. I need to know, and then maybe I can be normal."

Ryan took a moment to take in this information. "So I'm assuming you do know about the fires in your area," he said.

Abby's head sank. "Yes and no. When those happened, I have no memory, but I was in the area each time."

Ryan's face was filled with even more confusion. "But you remember what just happened now?"

"Yes," replied Abby, "it's been getting stronger, or worse. I'm not sure how to describe it yet."

Ryan opened up the car door and got out. He was trying to rationalize this to himself while pacing around the van. He stumbled a few times since he was still injured from Phil. Abby opened the door and got out as well, hoping to help but still keeping her distance from him after what he saw her do.

"They were going to kill us," she said softly, trying to explain.

"Let me guess, read their minds as well?" Ryan said snarkily.

"Not exactly," Abby reluctantly replied.

"Not exactly!" Ryan repeated back to her in a shocked tone. Abby started walking away. "Where are you going?"

Abby turned around. "I'm going to get food. Feel free to come inside once you want to have an actual conversation."

Ryan put his hands to his head, and Abby turned around and walked inside. There was no point discussing this while Ryan was still processing it. What just happened wasn't something a normal human being could comprehend.

The small diner was inside a rundown truck stop. Most things in Harmon were rundown now though. There were only two other customers. They looked like two old truckers, just sitting by themselves, getting something to eat while passing through the city, unaware of its declining state. Abby was greeted by a waitress. Her brown hair was tied to one side and covering her name tag.

"Just one?" she asked.

"Uh . . . two. He's just running behind," Abby replied as she looked out the window as Ryan continued to pace.

Abby was taken over and sat at a small two-person table by a small buffet. It was still the breakfast buffet. Abby filled her plate with sausages, bacon, and hash browns and then went nuts at the fruit bar. She sat and began to stuff herself. To her surprise, the waitress had already filled her coffee cup. *She's a much better waitress than me,* Abby thought. Abby finished her hash browns, but there was never enough potato. She argued with herself for a moment before going and getting more hash browns. Who knows when the next time was when they could actually stop and eat? Ryan walked in only a few minutes later and grabbed a plate. The waitress greeted him with words Abby couldn't hear. She pointed over at the buffet, and Ryan headed over to fill his plate. By the time he got back to the table, Abby had downed all her fruit and was beckoning for the waitress to bring more coffee.

"Okay, let's say for a second I accept this as a reality. How did Alexander know who you were?"

Abby paused the conversation for a moment while the waitress replenished her coffee and then poured one for Ryan. "I don't know exactly. He mentioned that our father talks to him. Maybe it has something to do with that," Abby said as the waitress got a safe distance away. Abby was so distracted by food.

"So maybe your dad knows where he is then."

Abby laughed. He clearly wasn't understanding the concept of who her father was. "If you want to interact with someone much more evil and dangerous than Alexander, be my guest. But I won't be involved." Ryan was looking visibly distressed again. Abby went to touch his hand, but he moved it away quickly. "I won't hurt you," she said, sounding hurt.

"You burned that guy's flesh off," he said.

"They were going to kill us, Ryan," Abby hissed.

Now instead of Ryan being the visibly flustered one, it was Abby. The blame and accusations were getting to her like she actively went out to find people to burn, come on. Abby got up and grabbed a takeout container that was on the table next to them. She packed up her food and then went back to grab more. Once her takeout container was overflowing, she put down some money on the table while giving Ryan a cold look. Abby sat in the van and ate, by herself again, her most comfortable state. She was frustrated with Ryan, not mad. After all, he finally found out most of her secrets, and he didn't just run away. Answering questions wasn't something she was used to either, but she liked Ryan and wanted him in her life, however long or short that may be now. While Abby sat in the van, a half an hour passed by. Police sirens began flooding the streets with noise. Ryan came out of the truck stop in a haste.

"They found the bodies. It's all over the news," said Ryan as he got into the car and motioned for Abby to go. Abby smiled. "Why on earth are you smiling right now?" Ryan asked.

Abby grabbed the exposed wires and started the engine again. "Because you got back in the van with me," she said as the engine roared.

Chapter 7

---

*A*bby drove back to their clearing among the trees, the one place they were safe before nowhere. Abby shut the van off and climbed into the back again. She sat with her legs stretched out, touching the other side of the van. Ryan followed.

"Okay," Ryan started, "I know I'm reacting badly, but this is a lot."

Abby nodded. "I understand."

"You do?" Ryan asked. "Have you ever told anyone this before?"

Abby recalled the time she finally confided in her friend. "Only Liz," she said.

"I didn't know how close you two were," Ryan confessed softly.

"Well, I haven't exactly been an open book," Abby stated.

Ryan's face lightened up. "Can I ask you a few questions? I know prying isn't helpful, but keeping me in the dark hasn't worked either," Ryan said.

Abby took a deep breath. She knew he was owed some answers. "Okay, but don't be upset if I can't answer all of your questions," she said. After all, the amount of questions Ryan had for her was probably nothing to the amount of questions she had for herself.

Ryan had so many questions but so little words. He stumbled around for a few minutes, like he was trying to get the perfect question so he wouldn't waste one. Abby sat patiently. After all, where else did she have to be right now other than jail if she was caught?

"Does it hurt?" he asked.

Does it hurt? Wow, Abby thought. "Umm, no," she said.

Ryan was at a loss for words. "Why don't you tell me when it started and we can go from there?" he suggested. His hands rubbed his eyes as if he was trying to wake himself from a dream or nightmare. Abby tilted her head and raised an eyebrow. "Please," Ryan begged.

Abby crossed her legs and sat up straight. "For as long as I can remember," she started. "I remember lying in my crib. My mom was lying on the couch, drunk, out of her mind. I would cry whenever she came near me because her head would fill mine with the scariest pictures and thoughts," Abby said.

Ryan's fear of touching her must have started to vanish because he had moved closer to her and was putting his arm around her. "You couldn't even be in the same room as your mom?" he asked.

Abby shook her head. "It drove me insane. I tried to kill myself twice before I was ten. I used to think that only the devil himself would mate with that woman. I just didn't know how right I was."

Ryan let go of Abby and looked at her. "Are you saying—"

"Yes," she cut in. "There's a reason Alexander likes living like the devil on earth," she said.

Ryan fell onto his back. "This can't be happening," he said in disbelief.

Neither Ryan nor Abby was religious or even knew anything about the Bible. In fact, Abby hadn't even read the Bible before. It just seemed like such a long book and a waste of time. Now that Abby had finally come clean, they could both use the information at hand to stop him.

"I should call this in," Ryan said, trying to find his burner phone.

Abby reached in his pocket and took it. "You're joking, right! We've come this far, and we know of at least one cop involved in this!" Abby yelled. "I'm sorry, Ryan, but that can't happen."

Ryan tugged at his hair. "Don't you think I know that! I'm panicking!" he snapped. Abby stayed quiet and let Ryan work out his emotions. "Okay," started Ryan, "we need to go to the library and do a little research."

Abby climbed back into the driver's seat. "On what?" she asked.

"On the devil, I guess." Ryan shrugged, clearly wondering if he had just gone insane.

The library was in one of the largest historical buildings in Harmon. It was empty as always. Reading had become something of the past like in most places. As soon as books became outdated, so did decent speech and behavior. The Bible, for some reason, was in best sellers section, next to books about vampires and wizards. *What's happening to this world?* Abby thought. Abby pulled out the Bible and found a seat at a table in the darkened corner of the lower level. Ryan continued looking for books up the small staircase on the second level. Abby began reading the Bible. It was pretty sad that her origins proved that at least some of it was real. Abby couldn't find anything that related to Alexander.

"Ryan?" she called as she walked up the stairs. "I can't find anything, so I figured I'd let the detective be the one to detect," she joked.

After a few minutes of no reply, Abby went to look for Ryan. She found him sitting on the ground with three books out in front of him. "It says here that the Greek god Zeus cast his evil sibling Hades out and imprisoned him in the underworld for one thousand years at a time."

Abby sat beside Ryan. "Yikes, I can kinda see why he's so pissed," she joked.

"While he's cast away, he can still communicate with his mortal offspring." Ryan continued.

"Oh, lucky them, or us, I guess," Abby said, realizing that might mean her.

Sure, Abby may have been visibly okay on the outside, but on the inside, this was answering a lot of questions that had been eating away at her. She always thought she was an uncontrollable freak, and it turned out that was exactly what she was. And it wasn't her fault in the slightest. Abby noticed some pictures on the library wall. They were photos of the town of Harmon. It was bright and beautiful. Everyone was happy, and children were playing in the streets. There was row after row of these pictures hung in the form of a timeline. The last picture was taken the year Abby was born. Each set of pictures all stopped that year as if that was the year that the darkness took over the city and everything changed.

"Why is it like this?" she asked, pointing at the pictures.

Ryan got back onto his feet and walked over. "That was a bad year," he said. "I doubt anyone would make art out of our city after that."

Abby was confused. "What happened?" she asked.

Ryan walked to a nearby table and had a seat, his legs still in pain for the events over the last couple of days. Abby followed, thinking that was what he was aiming for without words. "That was the day everything changed," he went on. "The leader of every gang in the city was found hung by streetlights. Any cops who tried to stop the violent progression were killed, along with their families, so after that, no one tried stopping them anymore, until you."

His eyes swelled. Abby could tell that this was when he lost his family, on the day she was born. "How did you live?" she asked.

"I hid for days while the bodies of my family lay outside the cupboard door. Now instead of remembering their faces, I remember the terror and smell of their decaying bodies," Ryan said. "And that's when Alexander took over. There were no longer multiple gangs in the city. Now it's one huge deadly gang with a leader that butchers children," Ryan said with untamed hate in his voice.

Abby walked back over to the pictures. "It's the day I was born," she said. "The day I was born was the day Harmon was overrun with evil." Abby blamed herself.

Ryan walked over to Abby and was about to say something reassuring in nature but instead said, "Hang on," and darted back to his books.

Well, that was sweet, Abby thought sarcastically. Abby walked over to see Ryan frantically reading.

"It says here that the energy is shared equally between mortal offspring." Abby bent down to take a look.

"So he needed to kill all those people then?" she asked.

"Well, he definitely didn't need to. But once you were born, he probably lost at least half of his abilities. So he made up for the power he lost by having a small army and getting rid of the people in his way."

It was all starting to make sense now. "I'm sorry," she said.

Ryan looked up from the books. "Sorry for what?" he said.

"I feel like I am partly responsible for your parents' death," she said. "If I weren't born, none of this would have happened."

Ryan got back up. "If you weren't born, I think we would all be dead right now. He would have already started an apocalypse or something," he joked.

Ryan may have been joking, but the more Abby thought about it, the more she believed he may have been right. "I don't understand why he didn't just kill me then," Abby said.

Ryan closed the books and picked them. "Once it's gone, it's gone. He wouldn't get your energy unless you willingly give it to him," Ryan explain.

For someone who had only read a few books on the topic, he was already becoming an expert. Ryan was still gathering a few more books to take with them. He was mumbling to himself while doing it. He threw the sling from his arm on the ground. It was just getting in the way at that point.

Abby remembered when there used to be librarians. She used to hang out at the library after school instead of going home. It became a routine for her. A nice old librarian would always have a snack waiting for her. She would sit the children in a circle and read them stories for hours. Now there was no use for a librarian anymore. Once the old one passed away, the city didn't even bother replacing her. Abby walked the interior perimeter of the building. She locked the doors so no one else would be able to interrupt them while they gathered the items they needed. A really old tube TV was plugged in on top of an old desk. Abby switched it on and turned up the volume. Lines of multicolored pixels crawled up the screen. Abby adjusted the TV and hit the top of it, knocking the picture into clarity. It was a press conference. Chief Doyle was leading it again, and there was a picture of a young girl in the top-right corner of the screen.

"Ryan, come here!" she called out.

Ryan ran over, tripping over a small pile of books on the way. They listened as the police pleaded with the public to assist them in finding the twelve-year-old Cassie Smyth.

"Another one," Ryan said.

"He's not a bad person," Abby said, regarding the chief.

Ryan looked relieved to hear that at least. At this point, he wouldn't have been surprised to find out that the chief was also working for Alexander. As Abby looked at the picture, she could hear the cries of Cassie. There were dogs barking. A faint image could be made out as Abby closed her eyes. She couldn't focus hard enough. It was like something was blocking her. The growling and barking of the dogs were the main thing clogging her head. She had never seen this type of dog before. It had an evil to it that was unique. Ryan and Abby walked back to Ryan's reading area. Open on one of his pages was a picture of the canine-like beast. The coincidences were starting to make her question her sanity more than she already did.

"What's that?" she said, pointing at the picture.

"It's called a hellhound. It says they usually serve demons or those of evil origins. They are more attracted to female masters," answered Ryan.

"What do you mean?" asked Abby.

Ryan looked amused that he was the one being asked for answers.

"I don't know," Ryan said with a smirk. "It says Hades doesn't even control them in the underworld. Their master is his wife, Persephone." He continued.

"Well, that's the type of dogs that are holding here," Abby stated.

Ryan looked at the picture and shook his head. Ryan continued reading about the hellhounds. "It says that they can come to earth and still for one hundred years to live out their purpose. Then they go back home for one thousand years," Ryan said. Abby grabbed at her hair, visibly upset. "You don't actually think they exist or that they're here, do you?" he asked.

Abby nodded yes. Ryan put his head down and sighed. He had already known the answer to the question before asking it, but it all just seemed so unbelievable. Ryan was now dealing with something he was never trained for, monsters and demons. One thing all criminals have in common, though, is that they can all be found by asking yourself one question: "If you were hiding from the authorities, where would you go?" asked Ryan out loud. Supernatural or not, Alexander would have to have some kind of a place to call home. Abby paused for a moment while thinking.

"Underground," she said while clapping her hand together once as if she had won a game show.

Ryan rushed over to the other side of the library. He pulled a map off the wall and laid it out on the table behind him. "Look," he said, running his hand down the diagram. "The city was going to put in a subway system but got the budget pulled. Now there's just some abandoned tunnels under the city."

Abby looked over the map. Something in her told her that she needed to go there. "I think you're right," Abby said. They picked the books and information they deemed useful and headed for the van.

Abby didn't even know where to start. On one hand, she wanted to go back to their safe place and wait until Ryan was completely healed so they would have a better chance. On the other hand, Alexander had Cassie Smyth now. The clock was ticking for the twelve-year-old. The map indicated that there was an opening to the tunnels in the basement of the Townsquare building, the one place that was unreachable and sectioned off by the police. *Right, police,* Abby thought. *With all this going on, I keep forgetting we're wanted,* she reminded herself. Both sides of the law were looking for them. Abby thought about what happened in Timesqaure, finding the body of the first girl, and the first time in the building when Abby had to escape. As she thought about her unpleasant experiences, Abby recalled the disgusting sewer tunnels that opened onto the back of that same property.

"Do you think that the nearby sewers might meet up with the underground tunnels?" Abby asked Ryan.

Ryan opened the map and examined it again. "I don't see why that wouldn't make sense. Even if it's closed off, it shouldn't take much to break through," Ryan answered.

Her mind went back to the moment she had to melt down and bend the bars to escape the tunnels the first time. Abby felt sorry for her boots again. That was a gross experience. They parked three blocks away in an old underground parking structure. No one was around. The youths who used to vandalize and rob people under there had also moved on out of fear for their lives.

Abby and Ryan traveled quietly on foot, making sure to take back alleyways and small roads so as not to be caught by the police or Alexander's men. The opening at the back of the Townsquare building would be much too obvious, and they could potentially be seen by the officers patrolling the grounds now that it was a crime scene. Abby followed the river along Timesqaure just out of sight, hoping it would lead them to the drain bars she escaped from. Abby looked back to see Ryan following her. He trusted her even after all the things he had witnessed. As Abby got to the end of the small river, she could see the bars leading to the sewage tunnel off in the distance.

"It's over there." Abby pointed as she picked up speed, forgetting Ryan was injured and struggling to keep up.

The bars were still bent out of shape. "You were lucky it was bent enough for you to get out," said Ryan innocently as he touched the cold metal.

"Yes, pure luck," Abby replied with a veiled joke.

Ryan had climbed using his good arm and grabbed the bars. Once he was steady, he struggled for a moment with an old flashlight he took off his belt. It was cracked, and a small piece of plastic-like material fell from it. He hit it against the bar, and it finally lit up.

"It looks disgusting in there," he said as he looked on at the mess that awaited them.

"It's not so bad if you just focus on the exit you're gunning for," she said as she slipped in between the bars. Ryan followed and focused on his footing. "You're in luck," Abby said. "There aren't any rats this time!"

Ryan nervously laughed as he used whatever dry parts of the concrete wall he could find for balance. Abby recognized the metal stairs she had climbed down when she escaped from Alexander.

"It shouldn't be much farther," said Abby as she motioned toward the stairs. "Those lead to the far end of the yard at the Townsquare building," she said.

"Well, we definitely don't want to go there," he said.

Ryan went in front of her and opened the map he had stashed away in his pocket. He traced the tunnels with his finger, trying to lead them back to the sewer system. His hand shook holding the flashlight down at the wrinkled paper.

"This doesn't make any sense," Ryan said. "We're basically in the tunnels now. They must have just incorporated the sewer system into the tunnels to at least utilize them somehow."

Sure, Abby thought. It was obvious Ryan was trying to rationalize everything because he was scared and freaking out a bit. His hands shook as he held the map, causing small folds to form in the paper. Growling could be heard in the distance. It was faint but echoed through the tunnels as it got louder. Ryan's face got almost as pale as Abby's.

"I think we're headed in the right direction," Abby said. Ryan gave her a glare of terror. "What? I was trying to lighten the mood. It's not easy. You try it," she said, joking.

Abby wasn't sure what was wrong with her. Maybe she was in shock, but she wasn't scared this time. The growl wasn't a threat to her, and she wasn't going to act like it was just to validate Ryan's feelings. She grabbed Ryan, and they ducked between an opening. Ryan's hands were still shaking with the map in his clutch, causing it to crumple and make noise. Abby hit the map out of his hands. The shadows of at least four dogs were visible because of the light they brought with them. Ryan turned out his flashlight. He was breathing so heavy that he had to cover his mouth to try and remain quiet. The dogs were finally in sight. They were huge. Their waists must have stood about five feet high, and their heads were bigger than both Abby's and Ryan's. The dogs' fur was as black as coal, and their eyes glowed an evil red.

"Holy shit," Ryan whispered. "Fucking hellhounds!" he said as he tried to back farther into the corner Abby pulled him in.

Abby shushed him. "They're beautiful," she whispered.

The hounds' heads jerked up as Abby's and Ryan's scent gave them away.

"Well, I'm glad you like them because it looks like you get to meet them," he said slowly, dropping his flashlight.

Chapter 8

A battery rolled across the stone floors and hit Abby's boot. The flashlight lay busted on the floor. The darkness blended with the black hair on the creatures, but their red eyes glowed and showed their focus on the couple. Ryan pulled out his gun, but Abby moved in front of him and motioned for him to put it down. Abby wasn't sure why, but for a moment, she thought that if she could try and communicate with them, they might understand that Alexander wasn't who they should serve. Back in the library, Ryan had mentioned that they serve beings with an evil background. What's more of an evil background than being the devil's daughter? She walked toward them in a calm, commanding demeanor. Her eyes weren't red, but they had a special glow to them as well. The dogs sat without command. It was as though they switched sides quickly and without thinking. It was just instinct. Abby slowly placed her hand on the closest hound's face. Its heavy breathing slowed as it became more relaxed. The other dogs lay down as they watched Abby befriend their pack member.

"Do you think they'll let us pass?" asked Ryan.

"Just go," said Abby.

Ryan stumbled his words as he went to argue, but Abby's cold stare was too much to handle when her eyes shone. Ryan slowly walked around the dogs while Abby continued to keep them calm. The hellhounds' red eyes followed him. They were interested but no longer threatening. As Ryan got in the clear, Abby slowly straightened back up and began walking with him down the tunnel again. As they looked back, Abby was surprised to see the dogs following them. Their eyes glowed as they trailed behind Abby. It looked as though she had raised these creatures whom she'd never encountered before.

A small doorway was lit by the same style of torches that were at Alexander's hideout in Townsquare. Ryan took his gun out and pointed it at the ground as they approached the door. As they got to the door, a gust of wind made the torch go out, and the hounds began to growl. *Wind . . . down here?* Abby thought. Something wasn't right.

"Shut up!" shouted a familiar voice.

A shadow came out of the now darkened doorway. It was Phil. His arm was slinged, but blood still seeped through the sloppy white bandage that covered the area where his hand should be.

"Couldn't get it reattached?" asked Ryan. Abby wasn't sure if he was joking or not but couldn't hold in the giggle anyway.

"No, there's a time limit to those sort of things," said Phil in a serious voice.

He reached for his gun and pointed it at the exact time Ryan did. As they stood at a standoff, Abby continued past them to search for Cassie. There were more important things to worry about right now other than a dirty cop. The hounds followed her as if they were her escort. There was a small bed with a young girl's jacket on it directly to the left as Abby walked in the door. Three coffee cups were sitting around the room, still mildly warm. Abby exited the room and went back to Ryan, who was still holding Phil at gunpoint and vice versa.

"They just left with her," Abby said to Ryan, unaware that Phil could hear.

Phil laughed. "Nice detective work, Ms. Briggs," Phil mocked.

Now that Abby's eyes had adjusted to the darkness, she saw Phil's state. His blond hair was filthy, and his perfect skin looked aged. The darkness under his eyes made him look insane.

"We don't have time for this, Phil. Where are they taking the girl?" Ryan demanded to know.

"I don't know," said Phil with a grin on his face.

"Liar!" screamed Abby.

Phil's left hand was shaking. It was obvious he still wasn't confident using it for shooting after Abby took away his right one.

"We have to go," said Ryan.

"Not until he tells us," Abby said while staring down Phil.

"You're not going anywhere," Phil said as he moved his finger toward the trigger.

Without warning or command, the largest dog jumped on Phil. His whole arm disappeared into the beast's mouth. The other three dogs jumped on him as they followed their pack leader. His screams didn't help him but just attracted more of the hounds as their growls could be heard filling the tunnels.

"Stop!" screamed Abby.

The dogs stopped their actions and stepped back a small bit while Abby walked over to Phil and stared at him, what was left of him. The darkness made it difficult to estimate the amount of blood, but looking at him, Abby figured there was a lot. She knelt and put her hands on each side of his head.

"Where is she, Phil?" Abby whispered.

Phil's breathing was very heavy. He was going into shock. Abby repeated herself over and over, whispering into his ear. Images of a small storage space or maybe an attic kept popping into his head. Abby saw the same women who attempted to get her ready for her meeting with Alexander. They were dragging the poor girl as they held her captive. Much more gruesome images followed. Abby was now seeing Alexander's plans for Cassie. Abby took her hands off Phil.

"You're officially no longer useful," she said as she got up.

Abby walked to Ryan and motioned for them to leave. "Shouldn't we call an ambulance?" he said.

What a good guy, Abby thought. He was almost a direct opposite of Abby. "I think the hounds are hungry," she said, and without any delay, the giant beasts jumped back on Phil. He was no longer able to scream, but the grunts and shredding could be heard as they ran back the way they came.

A small amount of light shone through the bars as they neared in on the exit.

"That was insane. I don't even know what's real anymore," Ryan said in a panic.

Abby kept running and didn't stop. Those were Alexander's tunnels. He may have been out, but his men would have been back at any time. As they reached the tunnels, Ryan didn't stop. He just dove into the river attached to the drainage system. Abby took a moment to recall falling into the same river and then passing out on shore. Now it made sense why Phil knew where she was and already had her description.

"Abby, come on!" yelled Ryan as he pulled himself onto the same dirt shore that Abby had passed out on. The snow was now gone, and just the dampness remained on the ground. Abby held onto the bars as she made her way toward the side of the drainage structure. She found her footing on the rocks leading up the side and climbed her way down. Ryan met her at the bottom. Abby held her cool as best as she could, but that girl's fate was exactly like the one they had found. Ryan was clearly upset at the image of his old partner being eaten by hellhounds.

"Phil, what did you do?" he said, falling to his knees.

Abby went to kneel with him, but he pushed her back. Before she could get upset, Ryan had thrown his guts up where he knelt.

The sun was still up. It was likely late afternoon. Abby hadn't been paying much attention to the time lately. They made their way back to the parking garage where they left the van. This time Ryan got in the driver's side. The bullet wound in his shoulder was oozing a small bit of blood again. He hadn't been given any time to heal yet.

"What now?" he said to Abby with a strained voice.

Abby looked out the window. "He's going to do the same thing to Cassie," she said.

Ryan looked at her. "I can tell he's your brother," Ryan said. Abby shot him a look of disgust. "He does that to girls, and you let dogs eat my partner alive."

Abby got out of the van. "You're on your own!" she yelled at Ryan as he ran after her, slamming the door.

"You have to admit this whole thing has gotten crazy," Ryan said.

"Then why aren't you letting me leave? Do you enjoy being in the presence of crazy?" Abby snapped sarcastically.

"Only when it's you," he said, grabbing her hand.

So cheesy, thought Abby. Seeing someone get eaten by hellhounds definitely wasn't an experience they could compare with anything else. And Phil was Ryan's partner at one point. Abby understood that it would probably be an odd feeling to trust his partner with his life one week and then watch that partner die the next week after he helped the man who killed his parents. Abby turned and walked back to the van without questioning him. Ryan looked relieved and ran to open the door for her, this time the passenger side.

"You said those were his tunnels. Shouldn't we just stake them out?" Ryan asked as he started the van.

"Once his men find whatever is left of your dear partner, it won't be that easy," Abby said. Ryan nodded, still noticeably shaken. "Do you want me to drive?" asked Abby.

"I've got it!" said Ryan sharply. He clearly needed to feel in control of something, and that wasn't going to be the current case at hand.

As they drove onto the street, Abby looked back to see the seven-foot stalker freak staring at them from the exit. Alexander must already know what happened, but it was obvious he was starting to feel threatened if he was sending the stalker again. Abby decided to keep this one threat to herself since they were driving away anyway. Ryan was already stressed enough, and Abby wasn't sure how much more he could take. Ryan was mumbling to himself about the case, how it was usually four to five days after Alexander took the girls that their bodies were found. Cassie had only been missing for approximately a day. However, getting her back sooner would be much better than later. Ryan pulled over into an abandoned old movie theater parking lot. Many businesses closed down after Alexander took over. The cost of insurance and hazard pay became too much for most of them. Ryan shut the van off and hung his head from both mental and physical exhaustion. Abby climbed into the back and reached around to pull Ryan back with her. He fell and lay on the floor of the back of the van for a moment. Abby leaned over him, her bright red hair gently sweeping across his face.

"Do you still trust me?" she asked.

Ryan reached his hand up and pulled her down to meet his lips. "More than ever," he said as he grabbed Abby and pulled her on top of him.

Before any foreplay would happen, Ryan's hands were already wondering. Abby was all for sharing another pleasure-filled moment together, but as she looked down at Ryan, his face went almost as pale as hers. His wound was now seeping. All the excitement had caused his blood to start pumping over time. He looked down at his shoulder.

"I must have reopened it when I jumped into the river," Ryan said as he started going into shock.

Abby could only think of one way to stop the bleeding, cauterizing it. "I can stop the bleeding, but it's not going to be pleasant," Abby warned.

"Do whatever you have to do," he said.

Ryan bit down on the sleeve of his sweater in anticipation before Abby had even agreed to do it. Abby put her hands over his wound. Her breathing quickened, and a small amount of steam came out of the area. The spot glowed under Abby's touch. Ryan's yells were muffled by his sweater as he grabbed the back of the driver's seat and gripped it with force. Abby took her hands away. The smell of burned flesh filled the van. The wound was cauterized, and there was no more blood being lost.

"I'm not confident this will hold it, but for now, you're not dying. You need a hospital" Abby said with concern.

"Just let me rest a moment, and I'll be fine," Ryan said with little effort. He was so committed to this now that he wasn't going to risk being caught in a hospital.

Abby got back in the front seat, while Ryan rested for another few minutes. It would be better to have Ryan's help while he was calm and relaxed anyway, but that wouldn't happen without proper medical care. Abby grabbed some of the books that were in the passenger door to pass the time while Ryan rested. Ryan had bookmarked many of the pages for potential information. She got back to the part that they had talked about at the library about the hellhounds preferring female masters.

"Do you think that's why they took to me right away?" Abby asked as she held up the page to show Ryan.

"I guess that's possible," Ryan said, rubbing his eyes, still gasping in pain.

"Is there another older historical building in Harmon other than the Townsquare building?" asked Abby.

"Just the library," Ryan said. He grunted as he pulled himself to a sitting position.

"But we were just there," said Abby.

"No, we were there while Alexander and his men were still in the tunnels," Ryan said. She turned on the engine and started driving toward the library. "What happens if we get there and get overrun by Alexander's men?" Ryan asked.

"Well, then let's hope my puppy friends are there," Abby joked, knowing her audience wouldn't be amused.

As they got to the library, the police presence was very noticeable. The whole place was surrounded, and Police Chief Charles Doyle himself was there.

"This is big," Ryan said. "Turn around," he said, pointing at the way they came.

But it was too late. Abby had already pulled in between the two cruisers and parked. She didn't care if they took her to jail; Ryan needed help. Besides, how could they keep her in jail now that she could bend bars? A small rookie-looking officer came over to the van and recognized Ryan right away through an open window. He opened the van without delay and knew Ryan by name. The rookie called for EMS workers to come take a look at his wound. Abby refused to leave his side this time even as they requested to transfer him to the hospital because of what looked like an infection forming in his wound. The EMS worker commented on how astonishing it was that Ryan was able to fight off infection and stay conscious as long as he did.

"How were you able to cauterize the wound? He should have bled out," the paramedic commented.

Abby shrugged, not knowing how to respond without giving herself up as a danger. Right before the ambulance door closed, Chief Doyle stepped in the ambulance. He was shorter than he appeared on TV. His hair was a sandy gray color, and his glasses rested on the end of his nose just like in the news conferences. The chief sat beside Ryan.

"Looks like you've been through the ringer, son," he said with a smile.

"Sir, Phil, he works—"

The chief cut Ryan off. "We know, son," he said. "We just didn't put it together until it was too late."

The chief was kind to Ryan and understanding about a situation that didn't even make sense. "This is Abby. She's the only reason I'm alive, sir," Ryan said as he clutched Abby's hand.

Chief Doyle smiled and nodded at Abby. "We all have a lot to talk about, but that's for later. Now we need to get you taken care of, son," the chief said.

He got out of the ambulance and closed the door, leaving Abby and Ryan with a paramedic. He hit the side of the ambulance twice, and they started driving. The drive to the hospital was quiet. Ryan refused to lie on the stretcher, so Abby sat beside him. The sirens could still be heard on the streets. Sirens were beginning to be the soundtrack of Harmon. Everything was so crazy, but for now, Abby's focus was the task at hand, getting Ryan cleaned up and stitched and then continuing to follow their leads and find Cassie. But at this point, most leads were going cold.

Chapter 9

---

*A*s they arrived at the hospital, Ryan's body was getting too weak to walk by himself. He finally agreed to utilizing the stretcher he was continually offered in the ambulance. Abby had a hard time keeping up with the stretcher as the paramedics were in a rush. Ryan's blood pressure and heart rate was dropping. A nurse stopped Abby.

"I'm sorry, hun, but only authorized personnel pass this point."

Abby wanted to push by her, to forcefully insert herself beside Ryan, but she also wanted to control herself. Unlike everyone else, being evil wasn't a choice for Abby. She was programmed to be exactly like Alexander, and each time she fought against her evil urges, it was an exhausting internal battle. Abby sat in a small waiting room right outside the door Ryan was rushed into that was labeled "Urgent Care." The waiting room was full of people, all upset, but one couple stood out. The male had just been released from hospital, and they were just sitting there and crying together. He had many wounds that looked defensive. They were the only people in the waiting room who had any kind of evil thoughts invading their sadness. As Abby focused and saw deeper into the thoughts, she saw images of the stalker freak. They hated him and wanted him dead. What else is new? She looked deeper, but it seemed as though they hadn't met Alexander yet; otherwise, Abby was sure he would be just as hated by them, if not more. A police officer poked his head in the door. Abby brightened up, thinking it was about Ryan.

"Mr. and Mrs. Smyth?" called the officer. The couple got up and walked toward him.

"You're Cassie's parents," Abby said. She tried to look down and cover up the slip, but their heads spun around.

"You know Cassie?" asked Mrs. Smyth as she looked at Abby with hope on her face.

"No," Abby said, "but I know of the giant who took her."

Mrs. Smyth's eyes filled with tears as she grabbed her husband's hand. It was obvious this was the first sign of hope they had received for their daughter.

"Is he in this hospital?" asked Mr. Smyth.

Abby shook her head no. "I'm waiting for my partner to be released," Abby said.

"You're a cop?" asked Mr. Smyth again, looking her up and down, questioning her appearance if she was, in fact, an officer.

"No," Abby replied, hoping they wouldn't ask her to explain things that were simply explainable.

"She's a consultant," said a familiar voice. Chief Doyle emerged from the hallway.

"No one believed us," said Mrs. Smyth with tears streaming down her face.

"I believe you," said Abby. "I've seen him, so has the officer I'm with. He's real. You have no reason to doubt your eyes."

These words seemed to mean so much to the suffering parents. "Thank you," whispered the couple as their escorting officer beckoned for them to continue following.

The chief sat beside Abby. They sat silently until a nurse entered the room with word of Ryan's condition.

"Abby?" Abby stood, staring the nurse down unintentionally. "Det. Ryan Finney is in stable condition. We'll come out in a few moments to get you." Abby nodded and sat back.

"Where will you and Ryan be heading next?" asked Chief Doyle.

Abby thought the chief would have been demanding answers at this point, for Ryan's trust in her seemed to extend to his boss as well.

"I don't know anymore, but the only way to find Cassie is to find Alexander," stated Abby.

The chief looked at her and then rested his head on the wall behind them. "Running into Alexander is a death sentence," said the chief firmly. "And I've lost enough officers this past week, let alone the past two decades."

Chief Doyle's frustration was understandable. And no one knew more than Abby just how hard his job must have been the past twenty years. A knock on the waiting room door startled them out of the conversation again.

"Ms. Briggs?" a small voice asked. "Officer Finney is asking for you."

Abby got onto her feet and turned to Doyle. "I've already encountered him once and lived. I would never put Ryan in death's path." Abby followed the nurse to Ryan, unaware the chief followed.

Ryan was already sitting up. "Want some Jell-O," he said with a smile while extending his hand. Abby ran to his bedside and hugged him. Ryan groaned, "Abby, wound!" he snapped with humor. Abby got off him and looked at his shoulder. It was covered in bandages. "They cleaned it and sewed me up good. I should be able to leave soon."

Abby's happiness to see Ryan was overwhelming. She was so worried she was going to lose him too. Her mind wandered to Liz now that Ryan was in the clear with his health. She couldn't help but wonder if this was the room she died in. As she was getting too far into darkened thoughts, Ryan broke her free.

"They said if we didn't cauterize it, I would have bled out," Ryan said to Abby as he grabbed her arm. "You saved my life again." Ryan continued.

"Detective Finney, it appears I need to be brought up to speed," said Chief Doyle as he entered the room.

"Do you trust him?" Abby asked, looking to Ryan.

"I'm the chief of police!" said Doyle firmly.

"And Phil was my partner!" snapped Ryan.

"If I have to place you in custody for your own safety, I will," threatened Chief Doyle.

"No, you won't," said Abby, getting defensive. An incident in a hospital would be the last thing she needed right now.

"Chief, please, she's the only one who's survived him. It could solve everything," Ryan pleaded.

Chief Doyle paced the room, thinking. "Why? Why and how did she survive him? These are questions that need answered," argued Chief Doyle.

"Because I'm his bloody sister!" yelled Abby with such force that the thick glass window cracked between the safety bars. Abby's anger seemed to be pushed so easy right now that testing it wasn't a healthy option. The chief froze, unaware of what his next words should be. "To answer the questions going through your head, no, I do not work with him. No, I don't know where he currently is. And yes, I can be just as destructive."

Chief Doyle took his gun out. Ryan went to yell at him, but before he got the first word out of his mouth, the gun was glowing the same color as Abby's eyes. As it glowed and got hotter, the chief dropped it. It only took the half second between falling from his hand and hitting the floor to melt. It hit the floor and formed a small liquid metal puddle.

"No one touches us," Abby said with her eyes finally going back to normal.

Ryan touched Abby's leg and startled her out of the rage that took her over. "Give me a moment alone with the chief."

Abby reluctantly nodded and touched hands with Ryan as she left the room, never losing eye contact with the chief since she now deemed him a threat. Abby stood outside the door but couldn't make out what the heated voices were saying. Abby could hear Mr. and

Mrs. Smyth crying as the officer's voice spoke to them. They were in a private lounge across the hall from Ryan's room. The Smyths had been informed that the search for Cassie was being called off as the forty-eight-hour mark was approaching. They were reminded of the lack of officers Harmon already had. Everyone seemed to have given up hope and didn't think she would be found alive. But she was alive; she *is* alive.

Now that no one else was looking for Cassie, Abby knew time wasn't on her side. Ryan would take many more hours before he would be able to just walk off and be physically useful again. After going back and forth in her own head, Abby decided that it was time for her to leave and stop this on her own. Ryan didn't need any more injuries. Abby got outside the hospital and looked around. It was beginning to get dark, and the streets were clearing as the police took their position to enforce curfew. *Where do I start?* Abby thought. She missed Ryan already. He was always ready with helpful suggestions. The only person Abby could think of who would lead her to Alexander was the stalker, the seven-foot bundle of joy whose job was to stalk and kidnap, it seemed. This time he would be the one being followed. The last place Abby saw him was the tunnels. Of course, he would be long gone by now, but it was a start. A black sports car pulled into the hospital lot in a rush. Abby watched as a young man got out of the car and ran into the hospital, his arm clutched and bleeding. Abby waited until he was inside and then slowly walked over to the car. The door was still ajar, and he had dropped the keys just outside the door on the ground.

"Thank God for people in a rush," Abby said as she got in. Abby turned the car over and shifted into drive. The owner of the car ran back out, clearly realizing he dropped his keys. He yelled for Abby to stop, but she skidded away into the approaching nightfall.

Memory wasn't needed for this drive anymore. This was the third time Abby had had to enter these tunnels, and each time, nothing good came out of it. The conversation between the chief and Ryan kept running through Abby's head, how she was the only person to ever have seen him and lived. Abby could tell Chief Doyle was a good man and a great officer. The thing was, he was trained to deal with the most evil people in this world. Alexander didn't fit that category. Yes, they were both born in this world, but only half of them belonged there. Even that half wasn't sure anymore. But the police were no longer dealing with something that could be stopped by guns, which Abby hoped she demonstrated to the chief at the hospital. As Abby drove away, a swarm of angered and evil thoughts overwhelmed her. They weren't her thoughts, and no group of people had ever been able to throw her off like this before. This was something much more evil approaching. And it was coming toward the hospital.

"Ryan . . .," Abby whispered.

Abby pulled a U-turn and raced back to the hospital as fast as she could. It had only been ten minutes. She thought she was safe, but as she got there, multiple police officers lay lifeless in the parking lot, including the owner of the car she took, who clearly waited in the lot. Screams came from the hospital as Abby exited the car. Tears filled her eyes. She wanted to leave but knew that wasn't a solution. Abby opened the doors. As soon as she did that, she could sense the same evil that was in her apartment. Her head became so full with evil thoughts that she fell to her knees for a moment. Nurses and doctors were scattering and falling over bodies that lay mutilated on the floor.

"Abby!" yelled Chief Doyle as he grabbed her arm and rushed her down the hall into Ryan's room. He shut the door and barricaded it. The chief had been searching for her.

Ryan looked as happy as ever to see Abby, not knowing her prior plans to leave and have a go at it on her own.

"I got us a car," Abby said to Ryan as she looked out the small window in the top-right corner of the hospital door.

"How did you do that?" asked Ryan as he ripped out his IV lines.

"I'd rather not say in front of the chief of police."

Ryan laughed nervously. Screams flooded their ears. It was the Smyths across the hall.

"That's Cassie's parents," said Abby.

"What? Her parents are here?" asked Ryan, confused.

"The police station is gone," said Chief Doyle. "It was burned to the ground this afternoon. We've been conducting our business here."

Ryan looked upset. His place of employment was burned to the ground. *Sounds familiar,* Abby thought. The screams continued. Abby cleared the door and opened it to listen, ignoring the chief's gestures to stop.

"It's him! Oh dear God, help us." Mrs. Smyth's cries could be heard.

"Stop!" screamed Abby again without thinking.

The evil was so overwhelming that her breathing started to become difficult. The door flew open, throwing Abby against the wall and knocking her out. The chief reached for his gun before he remembered it no longer existed, thanks for Abby. Ryan was now beside the hospital bed and grabbed his gun from the drawer of the small side table. He shoot the stalker multiple times. The giant stalker fell to his knees but got right back up. Multiple bullets barely slowed him down. Just like in Abby's apartment, he never spoke a word but instead growled like an animal or creature of some kind. He walked toward Ryan and the chief. The bed was blocking his way, and he picked it like it was a feather and threw it on top of Abby.

"No!" Ryan said with emotion in his voice.

The chief held Ryan back from running toward Abby and tried to shield Ryan with his body. They both stared up at the giant freak as he slowly walked toward them. With both hands, he grabbed their necks and lifted them off their feet. Movement from the pile of rubble distracted the evil giant. He let go of both Ryan and the chief as he looked away. He slowly turned around and moved toward the pile. Ryan and Chief Doyle fell side by side and remained on the floor while staring up at the sight. Out of the pile of rubble, a high-pitch scream deafened the remaining survivors in the hospital, including the giant stalker. The giant freak grabbed at his ears and roared with anger. Ryan and the chief covered their ears with both hands as they looked around the room, wondering what was about to go down. The bed was shaking, the glass on the windows shattered, and the walls began to crack. The damage was similar to that of a major earthquake. Chief Doyle rose to his knees.

"You're gonna wanna stay down," said Ryan as he motioned for the chief to remain on the floor.

Chief Boyle listened and fell beside Ryan again. Smoke filled the room as the cracks in the wall were filled with fire. The bed flew in the air with such force that the solid object smashed into pieces around them. As the smoke cleared, Abby stood there looking like a woman possessed. The evil giant opened his mouth and growled in a way that made both Ryan and the chief's skin crawl. Fangs were visible as he opened his mouth. Abby screamed again as he rushed toward her. She grabbed him around his neck and threw him against the wall. She jerked her head toward Ryan and the chief.

"Leave," she said firmly.

Ryan grabbed the chief's arm, and they ran out the door without any questions. The Smyths were just outside the door, watching as the events unfolded. Abby noticed the audience and kicked the door closed before melting the locks in place.

"You're done," she said as she ran at the stalker who was trying to get to his feet.

Abby placed her hands on his face and screamed as her palms glowed. Her anger only made her more powerful. She channeled all her rage toward him. They killed Liz. They tried killing her and Ryan and now a hospital full of people. As Abby burned through layer and layer of skin, the giant's growls turned into moans of pain. This sound excited Abby. Being able to kill evil took away a lot of its power. The more she burned, the clearer she could see the evil creep's thoughts. As soon as Abby got the information she needed out of his mind, she took her hands off him. The evil stalker was now just a faceless beast on a giant frame. Abby walked behind him and placed her flaming hands back on him as she snapped his neck. Alexander's first line of defense was no more.

Abby finally snapped back into reality after she heard Ryan slamming on the door. She wasn't sure how much time had passed. She never knew when this happened. She looked over at the door and stretched out her hand, and the glass shattered. Ryan reached in and shoot the lock multiple times until the door would open. Abby put her back to the wall and slid down it. Exhaustion set in after she used so much energy defeating the giant. The chief walked in slowly after Ryan rushed to Abby. Chief Doyle was holding Mrs. Smyth.

"Is Cassie's dad okay?" Abby asked as she tried straightening herself up.

"He's fine, just a broken arm before you distracted this thing. The officer they were with wasn't so lucky though," answered Ryan.

Mrs. Smyth broke down at the sight of her child's kidnapper dead.

"I know where Cassie is," said Abby.

Cassie's mother sobbed even harder at those words and buried her face in the chief's chest. It took the grieving mother a moment to pull herself together.

"I have to go tell my husband!" she shouted as she ran out of the room. It was as if this was the first time she had felt hope in a while.

"I just need a minute. Then we'll go get her?" Abby asked, looking up at Ryan.

Ryan looked to the chief for approval. The chief nodded as he looked at Abby and then back at her work. He was speechless, and it was also obvious he was an intelligent man who earned this position. The chief wasn't sure how to react to Abby, but it was obvious he needed her. Abby tried looking into Chief Doyle's mind, but the only negative thoughts were about Alexander and the disdain he held toward him for killing so many of his officers. Those thoughts of hatred toward Alexander weren't uncommon. Most people in Harmon had lost someone to him or his men over the years he had run the city. It was definitely time to take Harmon back and, most importantly, bring Cassie home.

Chapter 10

*A*lexander was now back underground, way underground, in tunnels that the people of Harmon had long forgotten about. Now that the giant stalker was gone and gave away Alexander's hideout, the journey there wouldn't be as hard. The journey back, on the other hand, that would be much more difficult. As Abby pulled herself to her feet and began leaving the hospital with Ryan's assistance, scenarios ran through her head. The age of the tunnels would mean that the structure may not be sound. Any loud noises or vibrations would cause a collapse. From what Abby saw in the giant freak's mind, the tunnels were crawling with his men. Alexander would be much more difficult to face than the giant, and Abby knew she didn't have a plan, just rage, pure untamed rage.

"There." Abby pointed as they got outside the hospital door.

The sports car she had stolen before was still there. Ryan ran to the driver's side, carefully avoiding the bodies that still scattered the ground. He dropped the sling, giving him more range to move. Ryan yelled in pain as he moved his upper body into the car and grabbed the keys. He got back out and opened the trunk.

"What are you looking for?" Abby asked, leaning against the car.

"Thought he might be carrying, might have come in useful," Ryan replied.

Abby looked in and pulled out a small six-pack of energy drinks. "Perfect," she said as she cracked two of them open and started drinking fast. Considering how useful guns had proven to them already, energy drinks were something to get much more excited about. "You don't have to come. You're not in the best of shape right now," Abby said, pointing at Ryan's shoulder.

"I'm fine. Besides, I've seen what you can do now." Abby paused at Ryan's words.

"Okay, but you haven't seen what Alexander can do," Abby said, realizing that she hadn't either.

The look on Ryan's face made his disapproval obvious. "I haven't? I've been missing a family three quarters of my life because of him."

Abby took the keys from Ryan and walked to the driver's door. "He killed them, but as harsh as this may sound, he could have done worse. And he could be doing worse to Cassie right now," Abby said sharply.

Before Ryan could answer, the door was slammed shut. Ryan rushed to the passenger side, clearly worried Abby was going to take off without him. He got in, and they drove off quickly. Abby wasn't sure if Alexander was her match or if he was even more powerful.

Abby and Ryan barely talked during the drive. You could cut the tension in that car with a knife. Abby knew she may have went too far with her words about Ryan's family, but she wasn't sure if her actions were also the problem. The people she had killed were all terrible people. They were all a threat to her or to others. Even Phil deserved what he got. He may have been Ryan's partner at one point, but he would have easily killed Ryan if Alexander had ordered him to. In her mind, Phil becoming dog chow was the best thing for him. Abby understood that Ryan had lost people and that the girl he had chosen occasionally looked like a woman possessed, but right now wasn't the time to be flaky. Still, the loss of Liz haunted Abby more than any others. The fear of Ryan pulling away terrified Abby. But she also couldn't be something she was not.

Abby arrived at the Townsquare building. The darkness made it look even creepier than the last time they were there. Two officers approached the car from behind. Abby looked at Ryan, and he pulled his badge out and went to speak with them. Abby waited for a moment until the tone of the conservation seemed to lighten before she got out of the car. She made eye contact with one of the officers but quickly looked away. Being friendly wasn't a concern right now. Abby started walking up to the building while Ryan finished up. The stairs were darkened by the night, causing Abby to trip and fall. As she fell onto the ground, a large growl rumbled the ground she landed on. She looked up, and both Ryan and the other two uniformed officers were looking on in terror.

"I think we're headed the right way!" Abby yelled to Ryan.

The other two cops could be heard offering to accompany them, but Ryan declined. Harmon had already lost enough officers, and they had no idea what could be waiting for them. Ryan ran over to Abby and helped her up.

"Do you think that means they know we're here?" asked Ryan.

"I think that's a large possibility," Abby said.

"Should we enter the tunnels from the far end of the grounds or through the building?" Ryan asked.

It was obvious he wasn't used to not having a plan of attack, whereas Abby was just used to acting without thought. "The yard. I have an odd feeling that some of his men might still occupy this building," Abby said as they made their way to the far end of the yard.

The opening to the sewer system was surrounded by mud this time. Footprints of large men's boots were all around it. Ryan took out a flashlight from his pocket and looked around.

"There's definitely been some heavy foot traffic going down here recently," he said, stating the obvious.

Abby lowered herself down first. It was darker than she remembered from the last time they were there. She walked along the side of the tunnel until something blocked her path. Ryan could be heard behind her hopping into the tunnel. As his footsteps approached, his light revealed a body in Abby's path.

"Holy shit," Ryan shockingly said.

Abby kicked the body over to reveal his face. It was a young guy, maybe early twenties, and his throat was almost black with bruising.

"This guy died a horrible death," Abby said, leaning down. "What are you doing?" Abby said, looking at Ryan.

"Checking for ID," Ryan said as he searched his pockets, looking for a shred of evidence to what happened to him. There was no ID, no wallet, nothing.

"It was likely one of Alexander's men," Abby said.

"Why would he kill his own men?" Ryan asked, confused.

"Just because I can see the evil doesn't mean I understand it," Abby said as she walked away from the corpse.

"So why is he like this and you're like . . . well, you?" Ryan asked, trying to explain his thoughts. "Does that mean your father favors him because he carried out his will, or does he hate him for posing as him?" Ryan's questions just kept coming.

"As much as I'm glad that you're taking an interests in me, I'm afraid I really don't have those answers. I wish I did because I'd like to know too," explained Abby. "Though I can say that the word 'father' implies a bond or relationship. I was never fathered by anyone," Abby added.

Ryan hopped over the body and followed Abby as she made her way deeper into the tunnels. She followed them like they did before and hoped to find something out of place to indicate another opening to the deeper tunnels.

"So is that why you're not evil and homicidal? Because you had no outside influences?" Ryan's questions continued.

"Possibly. It's odd. Most kids who grow up without parents end up on the wrong path. My situation made it the opposite for me," Abby joked, trying to lighten the mood as she always did.

"If we kill Alexander, do you gain his abilities?" Ryan asked.

"I'm not sure what you mean," Abby said, pausing.

"Well, if he lost half his power when you were born, then wouldn't you take his if he's gone?" Ryan asked.

"I guess that would make sense, but I wouldn't want them. I already have a hard time controlling myself. I don't need to double it," Abby said, trying to explain.

"Would you change?" Ryan said. He grabbed Abby's arm and looked her in the eyes. "Would you be like him?"

Abby's face was filled with anger. "After everything we've been through and seen, how could you ever think I could become him?" Abby said, pulling her arm away.

As she walked ahead of him, Ryan went to say something else, but Abby quickly put her hand over his month. There wasn't time for them to bicker like an old couple. Footsteps were coming their way. It sounded like one person who was very heavy on their feet.

"He sounds big," Ryan observed.

"I already removed the biggest one's face," Abby said, confused about who might be approaching.

Abby gathered it was likely another larger male working for her brother. She slowly bent down and picked a large rock that was by her foot. As Abby approached the turn in tunnel, she peeked around the corner. They were right. It was a large man wearing a full mask covering his face, not as big as the giant freak but still bigger than both of them.

"Does he look like a criminal?" Ryan whispered.

"Yeah, the balaclava kind of gave that away," answered Abby sarcastically. Abby was about to experience verbal diarrhea again. "Does me killing people make you want to pull away from me?" Abby asked.

"What? Is this really the time?" Ryan hissed.

"Is that a no then?" Abby replied. "Because I don't seek this out." She continued.

Ryan gave her an odd look, but before he answered, Abby went around the corner and was out of sight. A male could be heard letting out a small grunt and then a loud thud. It was only a few seconds for Ryan to catch up, but the coast was already clear. The rock Abby had picked was now lying beside the man with his blood coating it. His head was spun clean around. He switched as the life was still leaving his body.

"Would you like to check this one for ID too, or shall we keep going?" Abby asked as Ryan stepped over him while keeping his eye on him.

The tunnels seemed to be getting darker the further they went in. They were nearing the end of the tunnels that were actually recorded on city maps. The other tunnels had to be attached somehow. They hit a dead end. Ryan tried knocking on the walls to see if there was a hollow opening concealed.

"There's nothing here," Ryan said as he got upset.

"I think we're supposed to be going down." Abby knelt, checking for openings in the floor.

A small area in the right corner of the dead end had a slightly different texture than the rest of the concrete floor. Abby pounded on it. The sound echoed. It was hallow. Abby pressed her head against it to see if she could hear anything. It just felt warm. This was it, the entrance to a place that would get anyone killed—if they weren't traveling with the daughter of the devil, of course.

Chapter 11

Ryan and Abby found a crease in the concrete and started pulling on it, hoping it might lead to Alexander and Cassie. It began to give way, and they lifted with all their might. They could only get it a couple of inches off the ground because of the weight. Once they got it off the ground enough, they dragged the concrete off to the side and looked down into the unsettling darkness. The heat coming from the area was sickening as was the smell. Cries and growls could faintly be heard coming from the hole. *Were there more people kidnapped?* Abby thought.

"Holy shit, it's like we've found hell," Ryan said in shock and what appeared to be fear. It was obvious he wanted to be joking about something so crazy but was in disbelief he was living this experience.

Abby crunched down, looking for a way to explore their discovery. "Maybe," she replied to Ryan. "At least Alexander's version of it," Abby said.

Abby's eyes began adjusting to the darkness, and she noticed something metallic at the opening of the hole. She reached for it and realized it was a bar. It was the beginning of stairs. Luckily for the pair, their night vision had gotten much better after spending so much time running around in the dark after Alexander. Abby kept climbing down until the top of her red hair was out of sight.

Ryan whispered, "Abby?" as low as he could.

"Come on," she replied just loud enough so he would hear her.

Ryan reluctantly followed, climbing into the unknown. The climb down took what seemed like forever. It got hotter the lower they went into the unmapped tunnels. As they got closer to the bottom, a small amount of light shone up at them.

"Almost there," Ryan said to himself as he climbed down using his injured body. He was clearly doing better since receiving proper medical care, but Ryan needed a vacation after this, one long enough for his body to catch up on healing and sleep obviously. Abby jumped down from the last step. She waited a moment for Ryan and reached out to help him. "No," he said proudly, "I can do it." He fell from the last step and landed on his side.

"I never said you couldn't," Abby replied, this time helping him without giving him time to reject it.

The tunnels weren't what Ryan or Abby expected. Ryan expected dark, unused tunnels that were structurally unstable. In fact, that was his one major worry, a cave-in if a shoot-out happened before they could escape with Cassie. Abby just expected grosser sewage tunnels. This was completely renovated, similar to what Alexander did with the Townsquare building. They looked on at the godly, over-the-top decor. Everything was gold and red. The lanterns on the walls lighting the tunnels were gold. The gold continued with large statues of creatures Abby and Ryan had never seen before. The carpets were red, and the walls were painted to match. This didn't look like abandoned tunnels. It looked like a giant hallway to a royal mansion, a royal that was into creepy decor and being evil, of course. Giant canvas paintings covered the walls. None of them had any recognizable picture. They were just red-and-black scribbles from what Abby could see. Even though the paintings seemed like they didn't make any sense, they made their eyes ache by looking at them.

"Maybe the human eyes just can't comprehend this kind of evil," Abby said as she touched the painting in front of them.

Ryan looked back at the art once his eyes stopped aching. "Like when you can't put something in words. Only with this, you can't even describe it or give an image to it," he added.

Ryan grabbed Abby's hand. Abby wasn't sure if he was offering her support or if he was the one who needed the support, but either way, she accepted it.

The cries and growls Abby and Ryan heard before climbing down were clearer now but remained distant enough that they both continued without hesitation. Ryan still held Abby's hand firmly as they walked on in a slow creep. They chose to walk in the direction of the uneasy sounds, hoping they might find the cause. Ryan made sure to examine everything he passed as if it were all a threat, while Abby just bulldozed her way down the hall. Each light on the walls blew out as the pair walked by them. Abby noticed and looked back. Ryan stopped and followed Abby's eyes.

"What is it?" he asked.

Abby remained silent. She knew something bad was coming. She froze and listened. The area with the confusing paintings that was perfectly lit was now complete darkness. Ryan's grip got tighter on Abby's hand. After the experiences he had had with Abby lately, it seemed like nothing was far-fetched anymore. Abby wanted to scream or at least make a disrespectful comment on the red shag carpet they were walking on, but she stayed completely quiet, listening and waiting for what was going to happen next. The wall beside them had a similar painting to the others in the hallway except this one was much larger. It was about four feet wide and stood from floor to ceiling. It was huge. Abby and Ryan stopped to look at it for a moment. It wasn't anything special at all, yet they both felt drawn to it. *Why is this so luring?* Abby thought. It definitely wasn't the talent. *What would I know?* she thought as she looked on with Ryan. Her idea of art was ironic animal posters, so judging art wasn't something she could do.

"What is that?" Abby said out loud.

Ryan listened. The same faint cries and growls were off in the distance. "Nothing new," he replied, trying to remain calm and seemingly cool in this crazy situation.

Ryan couldn't hear it, but the growls and evil noises got louder in Abby's head. The evil thoughts and presence that were happening were unbearable. *Is that possible?* Abby thought while she looked at the painting. A painting can't have thoughts, or can it? Nothing seemed impossible anymore. Abby could feel a sharp pain taking over her head. She let go of Ryan's hand as she reached to clutch her head. The painting started to rumble and shake. The red paint within the art glowed and began to move. The designs and lines flopped around like snakes as they ventured off the canvas and toward Abby and Ryan. It was so beautiful what was happening, so disturbingly beautiful. Ryan was caught between assisting Abby and watching the impossible happen. Abby was now down to her knees on the ground from the pain being caused to her. Her head was flooded with the most unsettling images that no living being should ever have to have the burden of seeing.

The red paint got to where Ryan was standing and kept its form but seemed to harden. The long designs acted like ropes, grabbing Ryan, wrapping itself around both his arms and his neck. It tightened its grip around him as Abby watched on, unable to help him from the paralyzing pain she was experiencing. It pulled him toward the painting and up against the bare canvas. The rest of the design covered him, holding him in place. Muffled yells made their way into Abby's bleeding ears as the design covered Ryan's mouth and continued to harden and tighten. Abby's vision was beginning to blur as she struggled to keep her eyes open. She wanted to rush over and help, but she couldn't even stand. At this point, she literally thought her brain was going to explode. The amount of evil that was present felt like it was killing her slowly. Abby fell to her side, facing Ryan, who was using what little range of movement he had to bend his wrist and reach out to her. She tried crawling to him, but the closer she got to the possessed art, the more crippled with pain she became. As she watched on the painting, the portion of the wall it was hanging on flipped, and Ryan was gone. A plain red wall replaced it with absolutely no art. The pain subsided, but the aftereffects lingered, giving Abby a weakened mind. She lay on the red shag rug, unable to even lift her head.

"Ryan . . .," Abby whispered as she unwillingly lost consciousness.

Abby woke up not knowing how much time had passed. She tugged at her eyelids, trying to open them. Her eyes were still so strained and sore. As she eased her way into waking up, she expected to find herself captured, maybe even locked in a room again, probably chained up if they learned anything from last time. Part of Abby hoped it was all a bad dream that would magically be better when she opened her eyes and Ryan would be waiting to have breakfast with her again. Her thoughts were interrupted by a familiar sound, a deep growl Abby had last heard when Phil was being ripped apart. The growling was very close this time, basically next to her head. No, it *was* next to her head. Everything began coming back into focus. A familiar dark beast stood over her where she lay in the hallway. She was still facing the same position toward the now bare wall except now a hellhound was lying up against it, staring at her. Abby sat up and looked around as she rubbed her head. She was completely surrounded by the hounds. She counted eight roughly, but they kept moving and circling her, making it hard for her to focus on them. Abby reached out and touched one of the hounds as it brushed by her. The size was astonishing, and the fur was so rough it was kind of sharp on the ends.

Small cracks in the wall where Ryan was were now visible. *It did happen* . . . Abby thought. She wasn't crazy. The halls were completely lit again, making it easy to see all the details in the place. The statues of creatures that were already creepy were now complete abominations. If the sculptures weren't bad enough, canvas illustrations were done of the creatures' deaths. He made statues of his favorite kills. Abby's stomach turned, and images filled her head. She knew exactly who was here now. Sitting in a large red wingback chair that went unnoticed when they walked through the hall was the most hated man in Harmon, Alexander. This sight made Abby rush to her feet instead of taking it slow like she was doing. Dizziness came over her, and she fell against the wall that took Ryan. The hounds followed her moves with their eyes.

"Ryan?" she called out, hoping he could hear her on the other side of the wall.

"Ryan, huh?" Alexander snickered. It was no secret he enjoyed this kind of torture, probably any kind of torture. "Is that his name?" Alexander continued. "He's busy making friends with some of my men right now," he said jokingly.

"Why do you even care about him?" Abby asked as she rose to her feet finally.

"I don't. He was supposed to be a casualty about two decades ago, and my men love fixing my mistakes." Alexander walked forward, expecting to pass by his loyal dogs but was instead met with exposed teeth and snarls. The closest hellhound bit at his arm. The sound of its teeth snapping together when the bite was missed echoed. "I see the dogs have made a choice," Alexander said, staring down at them with disappointment.

The dogs began to surround their ex-master and growled with intent to attack. Abby took this opportunity to flee down the hall while the hellhounds distracted her insane brother. *That's my brother?* Abby asked herself.

Each hallway Abby turned down was the same, with very limited changes in the art but still along the same style. Either Alexander knew what he liked and kept it that way or he had no imagination. Abby kept running and trying doors along the way. All of them were locked, but she remained hopeful. *How big is this place?* Abby thought, exhausted while she turned down another clone hallway. She continued trying door handles, hoping to find one leading to either Cassie or Ryan. Finally, a door was unlocked when she got toward the end of the sixth hallway she ran down. Abby noticed creaking when she opened the door, so she adjusted the speed. The door crept open, and Abby walked in, closing it behind her at an even slower pace. It was too dark to see after she shut the door, but when she turned around, a string touched her face. She reached out and pulled it, hoping it wasn't a web of some kind. An aged light bulb flickered a few times before giving into its purpose. The light shone on a small sitting room. There were two chairs facing a dusty old tube TV. It was obvious the room hadn't been used in a while, yet it was the one unlocked.

Abby looked back at the door. The handle had been tampered with. There were scratches in the gold metal all around a tiny keyhole. Abby heard a noise coming from a small door within the room. Even though she wanted to walk the other way, her legs decided to do the thinking for her. She walked over and opened the door. On the other side was a small conjoining room. There was a small single bed that was so aged Abby wouldn't even trust sitting on it. There was a small dresser that was missing drawers. The old varnish had begun to peel and dusted the floors. Before Abby could continue observing the details of this new room, she was rushed and tackled from behind. She fell to the ground, and the attacker fell on top of her. Before she could even turn herself around, she could feel the attacker's body go stiff. A male fell off her and landed next to her with a loud thud. Abby looked at him in shock while she sat up. The handle of a large machete knife stuck out of his upper back. Abby got up quickly as the blood begun to pool and leak in her direction. She turned around to see who her savior was. Ryan stood in the doorway of the conjoining rooms holding a second machete.

"No way . . .," Abby said in disbelief.

"What are you doing here?" Ryan asked.

"Saving you obviously," Abby joked as she touched his face.

"You should have gotten out of here while you could," Ryan said. He pulled her in and placed his lips on hers. His hands traced her body and examined it. They stared into each other's eyes.

"What happened to you?" Abby asked. The image of Ryan being taken from her played over in her mind. That was something Abby never expected. Once you have something to lose, life becomes much more significant.

"The wall just switched sides," Ryan answered. "Then the paint that was holding me in place was just gone. I was able to fight off two of Alexander's men and get away before the others flooded my location," Ryan explained as if he was filling out a report.

"I've been looking for you for a while," she explained.

They continued to hold each other, but the embrace was cut short when a massive amount of gunshots could be heard within the tunnels.

Screaming and fighting began to spread from the tunnels Abby had just come from. Gunshots made explosive sounds within the underground structure. Dust and debris fell from the ceiling, making Abby and Ryan cover their heads and duck into the doorway. Abby and Ryan stood by the door to the hallway, trying to look out just enough to see without being spotted. A group of men began to storm the hall they were in. Their heavy footing as they ran rumbled the tunnels, causing some statues and art to smash to the ground. Abby watched as a disgusting statue smashed just outside the door to the room she and Ryan were in.

"That may have actually made it look better," she joked, pointing toward it.

Ryan looked over and snickered. As the men got closer, Abby pulled at Ryan's arm so they could hide back in the room. Ryan held her hand.

"It's okay. Look," he said. Their uniforms were clear now. It was police officers in full riot gear. Abby looked at Ryan in amazement. "I may have found a phone before I found you," Ryan said with a smirk.

He was saving her a lot for someone who needed her help. Ryan stepped out into the hallway first, and Abby followed. They were recognized and greeted by the officer who was leading the team. He moved toward them and removed his face shield. It was the chief of police himself.

"Detective Finney, glad to see you well," Chief Doyle said as he patted Ryan on the shoulder.

"Thank you for coming so quickly, sir," Ryan said, pretending not to notice the pain from his healing shoulder.

"Of course," Chief Doyle replied. "You've come closer than anyone else when it comes to nabbing Alexander. Every cop in the unit wants to be a part of the history being made." The chief continued.

The other officers waited behind their chief. Their knees were bent, and many of them acted restless. Their body language made it obvious they were men on a mission. The look of hope on the chief's face paired with the eager demeanor of the other officers gave Abby the confidence to keep going. She never once imagined she would have support of any kind, but now she had an army behind her.

"Have you found Alexander yet?" Abby asked.

"Yes and no," Chief Doyle replied. "That one's full of tricks." He continued. It was a vague explanation but likely the only one he could give. After all, how do you explain the unsustainable?

Chapter 12

The crew continued storming the tunnels. One of the officers in the first row gave Ryan a gun. He stayed behind a shield since he wasn't prepared and didn't have a vest. The officers and Abby kept sweeping the halls, trying each of the doors. The ones that were locked got busted down by the largest cop in the group, who stood right beside the chief. It seemed like most of the officers were flooded with passion to get Alexander, and recovering Cassie was falling to the back burner. There weren't many people in Harmon who hadn't lost at least one person they cared about to Alexander or his men, but there was no reason for Cassie's parents to join those heartbroken people too. The group encountered many of Alexander's men along the way. Abby was behind the first line of officers and enjoyed watching how quickly Alexander's men were being cut down. Bullets bounced off the riot shields and blew holes in the walls. As soon as his men were seen, the officers open fired. No one was being arrested today. *Oh my god, I'm part of a lynch mob to kill my brother,* she thought, making the odd realization in the middle of a small battlefield. At each tunnel crossing, more officers joined the swarm, and none of them had been hit at all. They had come completely prepared, thanks to Ryan.

The energy from the officers surrounding her made Abby feel confident and powerful in a way she hadn't felt before. The warmth that was sickening before was now getting worse. Abby wiped her hair back away from her face. The lights flickered at each end of the hallway they were standing in. Ryan looked back at Abby, and she nodded to him.

"Guys, something's about to happen," Ryan said to the officers, trying to prepare them.

Flames quickly erupted across each end of the halls like wind blowing across an open field. The fire stretched wall to wall, blocking them in where they stood. They were trapped, but the officers still held their guns and their heads high as they looked for a way out instead of panicking. Abby used to hate cops, but her respect for Ryan's unit was growing rapidly. These officers were clearly already expecting the unexpected. Abby wanted to help them so bad, but at the same time, she just wasn't ready for the whole police force to know who she was. The fire started to close in on their position. If something wasn't done soon, everyone there would burn to death.

Abby closed her eyes and whispered to her hound friends. "Help us. Help us. Help us," she repeated over and over under her breath.

Even to Abby's surprise, it wasn't even second before the area was crawling with dogs. Some of the officers pointed their weapons at the hellhounds, and a few even fired, but the hounds didn't even seem to notice. Bullets didn't seem to do much good with Alexander or his dogs. At least they used to be his dogs. The hounds were on the other side of the flames and looked on. Their expressions changed from their usual aggression to obvious confusion and maybe even a little bit of worry as they looked on at their new master. A batch of the hounds walked through the fire, and much like the bullets, it didn't faze them. The officers finally showed their first bit of fear during this mission and began to back down. They parted and let the creatures have the ground, submitting to them. As they walked through the crowd of officers, they ignored them, just focusing on

Abby, who was straight ahead of them. Their backs were eye level with many of the officers who remained frozen against the edge of the flames.

Chief Doyle removed his mask again and looked on at the creatures he'd only read about. "I thought they were a myth . . .," he gasped.

Ryan patted him on the shoulder the same way he did to him. "You might be saying that a lot tonight, sir," he said.

The dogs' fur absorbed part of the flames as they passed through them. Only two officers were brave enough to cross paths with the hounds and used the dogs' paths to get through the fire. One of the officers actually brushed against a hound while he tried getting by him on the fiery path. They disappeared behind the flames for a moment, and then a large crash rumbled the hallway. The officers threw a huge Victorian bench over the fire and motioned for everyone to come their way. Abby waited with Ryan and the chief while they watched the officers run up over the bench to safety. The two officers ran to their chief.

"Chief, we couldn't find any form of extinguisher nearby," said the officer, adjusting his mask.

"I don't think there's any need for that down here," Ryan said to the officer.

Chief Doyle and his officer looked around at the flames, confused by the comment.

"It would have been useful to control the flames," the officer said to the chief.

The chief looked back at Ryan with a look of agreement with his young officer.

"I think the flames were already under someone's control," Abby added.

The rest of the halls were much less eventful. The fire didn't spread after they got out but instead dissipated. The hellhounds followed Abby, much to the officers dismay. Abby continued calling Cassie's name each time the officers broke down one of the aged doors to the many locked rooms. The hounds followed and seemed to be understanding Abby's actions. They swarmed the rooms as

Abby called out and searched for Cassie. It seemed impossible. There were so many places to hide her. The officers went a bit ahead while Abby continued a more thorough check. Ryan went with the chief to the next rooms. At this point, the army of police officers were more at risk than Abby was. The loyalty the hounds showed her made her feel like she was at home. *At home, in my brother's hell?* she thought, right when she thought she couldn't become more of a freak. Still, the bond she developed with the hellhounds was remarkable. At least if it was *her* hell, it wouldn't be murderous and evil. *My hell? What's wrong with me?* Abby shock her head, trying to remove the crazy thoughts that called it home.

She went back into the hall and met back up with Ryan and Chief Doyle. They were standing outside a room just down the hall from her. The hounds followed, making the chief back up behind Ryan a bit. Either it was his first cowardly act or Chief Doyle had simply assumed that Ryan's connection to Abby would mean he had a rapport with the dogs too.

"No sign of Cassie," she said as she approached.

"No sign of Alexander either," Chief Doyle said as he peered out at the hounds.

"The fire was likely a distraction. I doubt he's stuck around," Ryan said.

"What are we going to do with them?" an officer asked as he exited the room he was searching.

Chief Doyle looked at Abby. "I suppose you would be opposed to euthanizing the lethal creatures?" the chief asked.

"I am, and so are they," she replied.

Abby thought back to when she and Ryan were in the library and reading about the hellhounds. If they came to each, they would be here for one hundred years, and only then would they go back home. Even if she wasn't bonded with the hounds now, they were indestructible.

"The best we could do is provide them with a place to stay under my watch. Gaining control over them is better than destroying them," Abby said.

Chief Doyle didn't look very confident about this proposal. "I'll have to discuss the details of this arrangement with Detective Finney before making any final decisions," the chief replied.

Four full hours had passed, but the search of Alexander's place turned up nothing. As the crew walked back the way they came, Abby noticed a similar indent in the floor that she and Ryan discovered. She walked over and got on her knees. She pressed her ear against it. There were no sounds, but air whistled beneath her.

"There's an opening here," Abby announced.

The officers looked to their chief before moving. "Well, go on then!" Chief Doyle yelled.

Abby stood back as the men tugged at the floor. "I found a seam!" one of the men shouted.

A large rectangle slab of cement moved as the officers struggled. Ryan went to Abby's side.

"Are you sure you want to go farther down after all this?" Ryan joked. He looked at Abby, expecting a reaction, but he stared on intensely at the progress being made. "What is it?" Ryan asked.

As the officers started to pull the cement block off, Abby could sense a huge feeling of hopelessness. The loss of life and the stench of death was overwhelming to her.

"Oh no . . .," Abby said softly.

The men removed to block and went back to get orders from their chief. As they decided on what order they would carry out and how they would handle the next floor of tunnels, Abby started to get frustrated.

"Don't even think about it," Ryan said under his breath at Abby.

But it was too late. Abby had already thought about it and ran to the hole.

"Hey!" an officer shouted. But she was too quick and disappeared into the dark hole.

"That's my cue," Ryan said as he walked over, tucking his gun into the back of his pants and began climbing down.

The officers followed right behind Ryan and stopped wasting time. It was a much shorter tunnel this time, but the temperature difference was still drastic. Ryan panted like he was melting. Abby didn't wait for the officers or even Ryan. As soon as her feet hit the floor, she looked around. This tunnel wasn't dark at all but had unflattering grocery store lighting. All the moaning and crying she had heard with Ryan made sense now. This was Alexander's dungeon, and from the look of it, when he knew he would be leaving, he decided to do a mass execution. Fresh bodies littered the tunnel, some in cells, and others lay butchered on the ground Abby walked on. She stepped over them, making sure not to touch them.

All the rooms and cells Abby passed were open or see-through. Of course, if he was going to kill all his prisoners and leave their bodies there, it was not very likely he had worried about anything else. At least that was what Abby thought until she came to an unmarked locked room. She tugged at the door without luck.

"Stand back," said Ryan, who was now standing behind her.

He shot the lock twice and opened the door. It was completely empty except for a large shipping crate. The sound of boots rushing toward them made Abby look up again.

"Your dogs are waiting for you up there," the chief said as he approached Abby.

"Why aren't they attacking?" another random cop asked.

"Because they aren't being told to," Abby said as she turned around and entered the room.

Behind her, she could hear Ryan filling in Chief Doyle on what they just found. The crate was locked when Abby tried opening it. She was unaware that a few officers had followed her into the room. The men worked together and popped the hinges off the crate, causing the heavy top to fall to the floor and alarm everyone. The box now had everyone's attention. Abby was the first to look inside.

"Holy shit!" she gasped, putting her hand over her mouth.

The girl lay there lifeless on top of plastic Bubble Wrap. It seemed like Alexander planned on going back but didn't have the time. It was definitely Cassie. There was bruising on her face, and her hair had been shaved off, but it was her.

"She's still warm," Ryan said as he touched the side of her face.

He lifted Cassie out of the crate and ran her into the hall. He placed her down in the middle of the hallway. The proper lighting made her injuries look even worse now. Ryan began light chest compressions as he wasn't sure to the extent of her internal injuries. Abby knelt beside Cassie and placed her full hand on Cassie's head. Her brain was still functioning, and her last thoughts were playing over in her head like she was torturing herself. Alexander's men made her strip down in front of them. They dragged her and forced her into the crate. They couldn't touch her because that would defeat her purpose for Alexander as she had to remain pure. The chief stood in the doorway leading to the room they found Cassie in and watched on, hoping she wasn't another fatality of Alexander.

Abby closed her eyes and spoke. "She's drugged. She needs IV fluids now."

Ryan looked at the chief's puzzled look. "You heard her," he said.

The officers all looked at Chief Doyle, who paused for a brief moment before shouting loudly, "Don't just stand around! Let's get this girl to a hospital!" The chief looked at Ryan, and they nodded to each other. Chief Doyle walked into the hallway completely and looked down the unsettling tunnels. "And let's get the hell out of here," he added.

The officers started running around, preparing to leave, grabbing gear they had dropped on the way. Abby and Ryan stayed kneeling by Cassie's side.

"This is a crime scene now. I want these tunnels guarded at all times," the chief ordered in a husky voice.

Two officers came back after their absence went unnoticed. They were carrying a small stretcher board and put it beside Cassie. Once Cassie was loaded onto the board and strapped down, the officers started back the way they came with haste, taking Cassie with them. Abby and Ryan lingered, taking their time walking behind the group. Chief Doyle was assisting in the transport of the injured girl. His voice correcting the two officers echoed louder as his annoyance grew with them. Some of the officers tripped over the scattered bodies as they ran as fast as they could to reach the ladder.

"Have you ever seen such evil?" Ryan said in shock.

Abby looked around at the loss of life. It was horrible, but yes, she had. In fact, she had seen much worse. Abby took Ryan's hand and rubbed his arm with her other hand. "Have you ever felt it?" she replied.

Chapter 13

---

etting up to the surface was like coming out from under water. All the officers were gasping for air. An ambulance was on standby, and Cassie was taken to the hospital with Chief Doyle by her side. Abby's hellhound friends had escorted them to the edge of the tunnel but stopped before stepping out into the open. She looked back and saw their eyes watching on. Just as everything was finally starting to calm down, Abby saw Alexander's men and what they were planning on doing. They always wanted to fix their boss's mistakes, and Cassie wasn't supposed to live.

"We have to get to the hospital," Abby said, and she jumped in a running squad car.

"Get out of there!" Ryan yelled.

"No, you get in!" Abby replied.

Ryan hesitated for a moment, and Abby switched into drive. "Okay, okay," he said, jumping in right before she sped away.

The officers didn't even notice their car leaving as Abby followed the distant ambulance.

The hospital was still a mess after the events with the giant freak. He and Phil were two people Abby knew had to die. Now the third was her brother. Abby and Ryan ran into the hospital and asked a nurse where Cassie was.

"They just took her into the ICU," they were told.

The nurse attempted to give them directions, but her voice faded as they ran around the corner, following the signs on the walls. *Finally,* Abby thought as she read "Intensive Care Unit" above a door. Ryan burst in, showing his badge.

"Where's Cassie Smyth?" he demanded.

"She's in there." A nurse pointed to a corner room. They both ran in.

"Detective Finney, how did you get here so fast?" Chief Doyle said as he got up from Cassie's bedside.

"Sir, we have reason to believe Alexander's men are coming here to finish the job," Ryan announced bluntly.

Chief Doyle's face changed to anger again. "That's what they think." Chief Doyle picked his radio and called for all units to attend their location.

"I can help too," Abby said, volunteering herself.

"They wouldn't understand," the chief said.

"You're the final act if we all fail," Ryan added.

But I wouldn't fail, so why go through everyone else first? Abby thought as she questioned their plan.

It didn't take long for the officers to start showing up in and around Cassie's room. Among the people rushing to Cassie's room were two familiar faces, Mr. and Mrs. Smyth. They ran to their daughter's side and held her before even noticing the commotion that was unraveling.

"Mr. and Mrs. Smyth?" Chief Doyle said without being heard. "Mr. and Mrs. Smyth?" he repeated while softly nudging Cassie's father. He turned around and hugged the chief. "Sir, we have a problem," Chief Doyle tried to explain.

"No, we don't. We have our Cassie. Everything is fine again," he said with tears in his yes.

Ryan chimed in. "They're coming back for her, and because of her condition, she can't be moved right now. That's definitely a problem," Ryan said bluntly. These events had changed his soft-speaking demeanor.

"Oh my god," Mr. Smyth said as he sat on the edge of his daughter's bed.

"The good news is that we're ahead of them now," Abby said to the whole room.

Cassie's parents held hands and looked on at their daughter. They were happy she was back with them but terrified that this wasn't the end of their suffering.

Chief Doyle was done taking chances. Two officers were posted outside Cassie's door, one was posted at the window, and regular patrols were done around the interior of the hospital. The chief and Ryan remained at the entrance to the ICU, guarding it and filling each other in the best they could. The best protection of all was when Abby planted herself on the floor at the foot of Cassie's bed. She sat against the wall and closed her eyes. The men could be there any moment. Abby stayed quiet, allowing the parents to reunite with their daughter. Cassie was beginning to gain consciousness very slowly as the IV fluids pushed the drugs out of her system. Her parents kept talking to her, hoping their voices would reassure her that she was safe now. Ten minutes of peace had passed when panic erupted again. Screaming was heard all through the hospital, no gunshots, just screaming.

"Are his followers here?" Mrs. Smyth asked while lying over her daughter to shield her.

"No, mine are," Abby said.

The officers at the door ran into the room and got out of the way. The two largest hellhounds that were in the tunnels had picked up on the scent of their master in danger. They walked in the room and quickly rested on the ground beside where Abby sat. Cassie's parents looked on at the giant beasts who were posing no threat at all.

"Are those . . .," Mr. Smyth tried to ask but couldn't bring himself to say such a ridiculous thing.

"They're my dogs," Abby snapped before any more questions could be asked.

It wasn't long before the thing they feared started happening, gunshots. This time it was cut short. Both the police and the hellhounds worked together. Ryan and the chief ran into the room. They both yelled at the sight of the hellhounds again. Ryan hadn't seen them in the light yet and thought his memory of how large and evil-looking they were was false. It turned out they were much bigger and much more unsettling than his mind could even comprehend. The only thing that calmed him down was looking over at Abby finally relaxing against the wall, and she stroked one of the dogs' long snout. As horrible that this experience was for everyone else, Abby seemed to be feeling at home. The more men they killed of Alexander's and the more they ruined his plans made Abby feel much more relaxed and alive. They were slowly taking away his power, torturing him the way he had tortured so many others. The nurses and patients who were screaming were now moved out of the path of destruction. Not one of Alexander's men got near Cassie's door. The screaming and growling seized, and the two armed officers who were posted at Cassie's door slowly entered the hallway. As the second one crept around the doorway, another hound brushed against his waist as he walked into the room with its two pack members. The cop screamed an emasculating scream. The hound sat beside the other two. More joined. Ryan stepped out to look at what occurred, and Abby got up and joined him. She put her hand out, motioning for the dogs to stay. It was a bloodbath. After what happened to Phil, Abby was worried that Ryan might break after seeing this. Instead, he started counted the bodies as well as he could. Some were fractions.

"Are you okay?" asked Abby.

"So far, this might help with your cause to save those beasts," he replied.

It was obvious he was trying to mask being in shock from the sight. A human mind should never have to be burdened with something so gruesome. Abby knew that the dogs weren't the beasts.

"Hellhounds only follow orders or do what their master wants. They did this because of me. I'm the beast," Abby said, looking at Ryan.

Ryan stumbled to defend her, but at least he tried. It was hard to defend something so truthful. "You're not a beast," Ryan started. "And—"

Chief Doyle cut him off. "Yes, she is," he said.

"Sir?" Ryan said with a shocked and offended tone.

The chief put his hand up and continued. "She's a powerful threat with powerful creatures backing her, which makes it so much better that she works with us," he said, patting her on the back.

"She's not a weapon," Ryan said.

"No, but in this declining world, she could become something much greater than that. She could be the one to change everything and tip the scales in the favor of good instead of evil, an unlikely savior."

Chief Doyle expressed such emotion to them with a gleeful wonder in his eyes. With everything that was happening, the three of them didn't notice that their conversation was no longer private. Most officers had returned back now to check in with the chief, and Cassie's parents were also peeking out into the hall with a hopeful look in their eyes. A few nurses had returned to their charge desk and became emotional at the thought of this free world as well. *No pressure*, Abby thought.

"I guess keeping my crap on the down low is over now, eh?" Abby whispered to the chief.

The trio slowly walked back into the room and shut the door. Whispers began as soon as they turned their backs. The chief is normally so rational, but he was going to get the whole city's hopes up. This is what desperation looks like.

"What was that?" Abby snapped at the chief.

"He's right, Abby," Ryan said. Abby huffed and looked away. "It's possible you're the only person that can stop Alexander, and if his death ends up being in the public eye, there's going to be no way we can cover up everything," Ryan explained.

Abby knew it was true. She would just have to hope that her full identity wasn't made totally public. Abby looked around the room. Before she could resort to anger like she was used to, she noticed something. The look of terror on Mr. and Mrs. Smyth had vanished. Mrs. Smyth was talking to Cassie, who was now trying to open her eyes and look at her mom. And Mr. Smyth was talking to an officer while petting a very big hellhound he was terrified of moments earlier. Just then, Abby realized something, something she should have known her whole life, but she was clouded with rage. It doesn't matter how evil something appears to be or even how evil they were *made* to be. Actions are what matters. Out in the hall, the officers were feeding the hounds meat from uneaten sandwiches on food trays and touching them with amazement on their faces instead of fear. If the hellhounds can become accepted by regular people after they were no longer evil, then maybe anyone could.

Everyone was sitting quietly for a few moments before a man joined the crowd in the room. His white coat made it obvious he was a doctor.

"I'm going to need at least half of you people to clear out and give me space with my patient," he ordered.

The extra officers all cleared out. Abby could hear them whispering about where the cafeteria was. The doctor had been staring eye level, requesting humans to leave, without noticing the beasts at Abby's feet. Abby pointed, and the hounds quickly scurried out of the room without a sound so they wouldn't throw the doctor off his game before treating Cassie. Ryan stood near the corner of the room with Chief Doyle, close enough to Cassie's bed that they could overhear some of what the doctor was saying. Abby stood alone by the door. She wanted a yes or no as to whether Cassie was okay, not a bunch of details that only health-care professionals need to know. A look of relief swept over Mr. and Mrs. Smyth's faces. Ryan slowly walked over to Abby when Chief Doyle joined them at the bed for his first experience of joy in a long time.

"Her vocal cords are burned and layered with scar tissue. It's going to take a few weeks for that to heal. Once she's fully conscious, we're going to try written communication," Ryan informed Abby. So there was a still a while to wait.

Cassie regained consciousness and, with the support of her parents, began communicating with Ryan and Chief Doyle on a small notepad. Abby looked on aggressively, waiting. She found her, and she was safe. Why couldn't she help us now? This was why Abby never went to hospitals, no bedside manners. Once she realized what she was doing, she stopped and walked into the wall. Abby shook her head at herself. Even after all this, she still had a short fuse. Abby looked around at the hall. Most of the area was still evacuated in case another incident happened. Even the dogs seemed to have left for now. Abby went for a walk around the halls, thinking. Alexander had moved on by now, but Abby had no idea where. His tunnels were the best spot for him, but those were totally blocked off, and Chief Doyle had been in frequent contact with the officers posted so he hadn't tried returning. He had already lost his biggest and strongest man whom he used to kidnap and murder whoever he needed. He lost Phil, who was hopefully the only crooked cop on his payroll. He has also lost countless men now, and his loyal hellhounds had abandoned him. Now that he had lost so many resources, he didn't have many places to go. Abby thought about something they would never consider him doing, going back to where it began, the Townsquare building. It used to be the most beautiful building in Harmon and filled with the most history other than the library. Now the library was burned to the ground, and the Townsquare building was damaged, dark, and dingy. Those were cons that could only be turned into pros for Alexander. *Would he actually go back there?* Abby thought.

When Abby got back to the room, Ryan was standing by the door, looking as though he had been waiting for her.

"Did you find anything out?" she asked, holding back her request to revisit the Townsquare building.

Ryan handed Abby two small pieces of paper. "This is all we could get out of her right now," Ryan replied, looking over at Cassie, who was asleep and resting now.

One of the pieces of paper had a drawing of all the body parts he injured on her and a picture of a kidney he had already removed from her. The other had one sentence on it. Ryan had asked if she knew where Alexander had planned on taking her, and the paper read, "He kept saying he was taking me home." Abby paused, looking alarmed. Before Ryan noticed the look on her face, he shared the assumption that he was probably just lying, saying he was taking her back home to her parents. Abby thought back to when she woke up in the old Townsquare building. The women who came in to prepare her to meet with Alexander specifically said, "Welcome home." Abby didn't want to sneak away again, but if this was actually where Alexander was hiding again, then going near this fight could be lethal for any regular humans because Abby wasn't planning on letting him walk away.

"I have to go do something," Abby said to Ryan.

"What do you mean? We have to stay together. We're so close," Ryan replied.

"I know, and I'll be back," Abby said.

But Ryan looked hurt, like she was abandoning him at the worst time. "What happens if we need help? You know guns do nothing to him," Ryan said as he was tapping the gun that was tucked into the side of his pants. Abby went silent for a moment and shut her eyes. "What are you doing?" Ryan asked, clearly annoyed that his protest went unheard.

As Abby opened her eyes, one of her big hounds walked around the corner by the couple and straight into Cassie's room. "I was getting you help just in case," Abby said. She walked back over to Ryan and embraced him.

"I love you, Abby," Ryan said as if they were parting for a final time. "Everything I love turns to ash." Abby sighed, fearing that she had already sealed his fate by including him in this fight against evil.

Chapter 14

---◆---

*T*he day came and went without Abby even noticing. It was now nightfall again. Curfew was still in effect, but because the police were busy doing other things, no one was around to enforce it. The regular public were still off the streets, though, out of fear for their safety. The sound of glass shattering and the roaring car alarms indicated that some lone criminals felt secure enough to come out now though. No real threat there, Abby decided to walk down the street to find a way to Townsquare since it was all the way across the city, but she didn't feel up to grabbing a police car again. None of the officers even noticed last time, but police cars were just too noticeable, and it might tip off the very person she was trying to find.

Abby wandered down the street. She passed a lit window and looked in the reflection. It was painfully obvious she hadn't been taking care of herself the last few days. Her long red hair was tangled in some areas with a small amount of dirt sprinkled through it. Her favorite thigh-high boots were covered in mud and scuffs. Her jeans were ripped and dirty. *At least my coat looks great still*, she thought as she ran her fingers through her hair. The sound of smashing glass snapped her out of this sudden self-judgment. Abby looked around and saw a figure breaking into a car across the street. It was parked outside an old shutdown pawnshop. Abby walked across the street. By the time she got over there, she noticed that the figure was a middle-aged male. He had broken the window and opened the door, now sitting in the driver's seat.

"Whatcha doing?" she said to the car thief.

The man got out of the car and stood facing Abby. He wore skinny jeans and bright yellow shoes. Abby couldn't help but smile at the sight.

"Back off," he said, holding a tire iron.

Abby walked up to the man without losing eye contact. The man swung, but Abby caught the iron. She yelled from the pain that the hard impact caused her hands. The tire iron glowed and got extremely hot. The car thief tried to let go, but Abby bent the iron tightly around his wrists. She quickly got into the car he was attempting to steal. She looked under the driver's side to find that he had already completed hot-wiring the car. She rubbed the two wires together, and the old car started without a problem.

"Thanks for your help," Abby said as she skidded away. She looked in the rearview mirror to see the car thief heading toward the hospital. "I'm sure the police are going to love meeting him," she said before she started focusing on the road in front of her.

The road ahead was darker than usual. The streetlights were all smashed. One thing was recognizable on the street moving. A single hellhound was walking the same way Abby was driving. *Why is he out in the open like this?* Abby thought with more concern for the hound's safety than anyone on the street. She slowed down the old car and reached over to pull the old manual handle. The door swung open.

"Hey!" Abby yelled to the large beast.

Its ears perked up, and it ran toward the car like a regular dog excited to see its family. But once it got in the car and jumped to the back, Abby was made very aware that these weren't just dogs. Every time the hound took a breath or let it out, a slow unnerving growl echoed out. It was constant. Blood soaked the fur around the hound's mouth and down his chest, likely from eating more of Alexander's men, hopefully just Alexander's men. Its eyes glowed red, and it felt like it could stare right into her mind.

"How many people have you eaten?" she asked the hellhound out loud, fully aware that the beast couldn't answer. "I know you can't talk, but there's no one else here to listen." She continued. As they drove into the heart of Harmon, Abby continued talking to the hellhound, and it did show signs that it was listening like every normal dog. Its ears perked, its head tilted, and it was always looking at her. "I've been thinking about getting a pet for a while now. I was thinking about a cat, but I don't think anything else could compare after meeting you, guys." She continued. "Liz liked cats. She sold me on the idea," Abby confided in the animal.

The hellhound stood. The old car made noises that made Abby worry it was about to fall apart. She focused on the car for a moment, and when she looked in the rearview mirror again, the hound's face was right beside her. As it turned to face her, she could feel its hot breath on the side of her face. It opened its mouth and licked her up the side of the cheek, leaving a mixture of saliva and blood behind on her pale skin.

"I appreciate the gesture but gross," Abby said as she used her sleeve to wipe away some of the residue. *Now my jacket looks like the rest of me,* she thought.

Abby was so distracted that she almost didn't notice she was about to pass her apartment building. This corner looked so different without Duffy's bar or the Busy Mart. The other tenants in the building seemed to be inside, obeying curfew. Some had even gone as far as boarding up their windows now. If only they knew what was actually happening, a little wood and some nails weren't going to help anyone. Abby knew she had to get to Townsquare, but she was already almost there, and she hadn't been home in over a week. A change of clothing and her shower were calling her.

"You need to wash your mouth badly," she said, looking at the hound.

Abby pulled into a small parking lot behind her building and turned off the car. She waited, looking around at the darkness for a while to assure she wouldn't be in for any more surprises.

Abby and the hound slammed the door to the apartment building after them and ran down the hall toward her apartment. The hound seemed to mirror Abby's actions and followed her. She reached into the pocket of her jeans and struggled for a moment to open the door. It had been bent after the break-in. A scream echoed through the hallway. Abby swung around to find her older neighbor standing just outside her door. Her eyes were locked on the hellhound and filled with terror. Blood still dripped off its fur and from its long fangs. She ran inside and locked her door. Abby walked toward it, about to knock, as she heard her beginning a call to the police.

"I guess Ryan will know where to find us," Abby said sarcastically to the hound.

She walked back to her door and let herself in. The hound followed behind her. Abby looked around at the place she used to lock herself into. It was so small. She pointed for the hound to get into the shower and began doing something she never dreamed would ever happen. She bathed a hellhound. She lathered its rough fur with soup and sprayed water into its mouth. The hound reacted like most dogs with excitement, confusion, and lots of tail-wagging, which from a hellhound can be painful. The speed and roughness of its fur caused whip marks up Abby's arms.

"Okay, go," she said, helping the hound out of the tub as its giant paws were sliding.

Abby looked at the shower she was going to step into, blood and long black fur. She dumped soap into the tub and let the overhead shower wash it away. Abby walked out of the bathroom back into the tiny bachelor to find the wet hound lying on its back in the middle of the floor. It was acting so much like a regular dog Abby couldn't help but rub its stomach. She walked over to her closet and picked out a new pair of jeans, a black tank top, and her favorite black lace sweater and set them on the bed. She opened a draw in an aged dresser and picked out a leopard print bra and underwear set and placed those with her clean clothes. Then she grabbed her boots and took them back into the bathroom with her. She ran them under the water, removing everything except the scuff marks.

"I'll find a way," she mumbled as she ran her thumb across the scratched leather.

She quickly wiped off the leftover water from the boots and set them on the counter just outside the bathroom door.

Abby stripped down once she noticed the shower was clean now. She got in and went directly under the water without hesitation. Steam filled the tiny bathroom, fogging up the small mirror over the sink. She soaked her hair and was relieved to see that she still had some shampoo left. She lathered her hair with much more of the product than needed and moaned. It had been a while. The steaming hot water trickled down her body, leaving goose bumps on her skin. She was thrilled at the sight of her strawberry-scented bodywash on the corner ledge of the tub. She grabbed a washcloth from a small towel rack just outside of the shower. She filled the cloth with her bodywash and rubbed her entire body. Lastly, she rubbed between her legs and rubbed herself clean. She trembled as she brushed past her sensitive bits. Abby rinsed the washcloth and placed it on the side of the shower. She cupped water in her hand and splashed between her legs.

There is no time to be aroused, Abby thought. She covered her hair in conditioner and shaved where she needed to. She stood under the shower and rinsed her hair. She ran her hands down her body, assisting the water in moving soap. She slipped her hand between her legs again and touched herself to make sure the soap was gone, but after it was gone, she kept touching herself. Abby leaned against the wall of the shower and circled her clit with her fingers. It was so swelled and sensitive. *Maybe this will relax me for later,* Abby thought, trying to justify it to herself. Just as she started rubbing and heading toward total release, she heard her door open and close. And then the door to the bathroom opened. The hellhound never growled, so she didn't think it was anyone threatening.

"Abby?" Ryan's voice matched the figure outside the shower curtain.

"Just a minute," she said, straining. She couldn't stop touching herself because of how close she was.

"Should I join you?" he asked. Abby pulled the shower curtain open. Ryan looked at her, full naked with one hand in her groan. "Wow," he said as he stripped down as fast as he could and joined her.

He got in so fast that he almost fell, and they laughed. The laugh was cut short when he kissed her with incredible power. Her hand was replaced by his. He messaged her clit with his thumb, and the sensitive clump of nerves began to throb. He forced his index and middle finger deep inside her while his thumb continued rubbing her clit.

"Yessss," Abby moaned as she fell into him.

Her legs began to shake, and Abby actually screamed out in pleasure. Abby squirted all over Ryan's hand, and the moisture joined with the rest of the water in the shower. He finished the job she started. Abby went to get on her knees to show Ryan just how thankful she was but was instead picked and thrown over his shoulder. Abby yelled and laughed. He burst through the bathroom door, and their nude bodies fell onto her bed, just missing the sleeping hellhound in the middle of the floor. Ryan landed on top of her. His swelled and twitching erection poked into her hip. Ryan grabbed Abby's hands and pinned them over her head. Abby could feel the tip of his penis edging toward her opening as he lined his hips up with hers. Without any delay, he thrust inside her. Abby wrapped her legs around him as she accepted his full length. She was soaked and not from the shower. It had been a few days. So much like Abby, it didn't take Ryan long to cum. He thrust as hard and as deep as Abby could take it. Her pussy stretched around his cock and gripped it. Ryan's thrusts began to get faster and less voluntary until he started to moan loudly. The final thrust was so deep and hard that Abby yelled. Ryan didn't move and stayed deep inside her as he yelled out. She could feel his cock pumped cum deep inside her. Ryan slowly pulled out of her and fell on the bed. Abby went into the bathroom again and quickly cleaned herself up. She came back and lay down.

"That was amazing," she said, realizing how cliché it sounded.

"This needs to be a nightly thing," Ryan said.

They kissed in agreement and lay there for a moment. Abby had never felt so satisfied. Abby wanted to spend all day fucking, but like most good things in life, they had to end, and they had to snap back into reality. As they lay there, screams could be heard coming from the streets. Abby and Ryan looked at each other and had one more quick kiss before they started getting ready.

The hellhound was woken by the screams and was at the door, sharing Abby's curiosity. Ryan got ready fast and went to take a look. Abby got ready as fast as she could. The lace on her underwear brushed against her parts that Ryan had just sent into overdrive. She trembled from how sensitive they were and then smiled from the memory of their animalistic rough sex. She ignored the screams like she ignores a lot of the thoughts in her head. *I wonder,* she thought. Abby reached into her underwear and started rubbing herself fast again. It sent her into a fast orgasm because of how swelled she already was. Not as explosive as the one Ryan gave her, but this one gave her a calming effect that made it easy for her to focus again. Ryan came in as Abby was putting her pants on.

"I didn't see anything. We should probably go check it out," he said. Abby grabbed her keys and went to leave with him. "I feel like you did something while I was gone," he said, smiling.

"Don't worry, next time, we'll do it together again," she said, longing for his tongue.

Okay, focus, she thought. Ryan definitely seemed to feel more connected to her after each time they shared their bodies. He got calmer and touched her a lot more even while they walked. The hellhound followed a few feet behind them but never left them. They got outside into the parking lot, and Abby pointed at the old car she had grabbed. Ryan laughed at the sight of the scrapper and pointed to a new unmarked police car he came in.

"Makes sense," Abby said as they started walking toward Ryan's car.

"Is that thing expecting to come in the car with us?" Ryan said, pointing at the huge beast walking behind them.

"Don't worry, he had a bath," Abby said with a smirk.

Ryan looked at the hellhound, its eyes glowing in the night. "Where are the others?" he asked, hoping they weren't about to follow.

"I actually don't know. I figured your coworkers were still hanging out with them," Abby replied.

Ryan opened the back door, and the hound dove in. The car shook from its weight. Abby got in the passenger side and was joined by Ryan. He put his hands on the steering wheel, and they stayed there for a moment, thinking about their previous dialogue. They started laughing.

The screams from the public seemed to faint now. Abby and Ryan drove away from their building without even stopping at his place. They were unusually calm for people who had witnessed the amount of evil they had. Abby reached out and grabbed Ryan's hand while he drove. He was the reason she was this calm, and he was the reason she finally had something to live for. As they drove on, it became apparent that people were fleeing away from the center of the city. The closer Ryan and Abby got to Townsquare, the more chaos they witnessed. Fires were spreading between buildings and getting out of control. As Abby focused on the buildings crashing beneath the flames, she felt the car jerk to one side and come to a fast halt.

"What happened?" she said quickly.

"I don't know," Ryan said with his eyes locked on the road they were heading toward.

The concrete had huge cracks, and steam poured out of them. Cars and other debris had sunk into them and stuck out partway.

"That could have been bad," Abby said, looking on.

Going on foot was the only way now.

Chapter 15

---◆---

 yan and Abby quickly walked through the city toward
Townsquare, making sure to take note of all possible
dangers around them. Luckily, they were forced to ditch the car only
a few blocks from their destination. They continued with haste until
Abby stopped in her tracks beside him. Abby could hear it clear,
but as Ryan followed Abby's lead and slowly crept closer, he could
hear howling coming from the openings in the separated earth. The
hellhound that was with them responded and matched the howls.
He ran quickly toward the crack. Abby watched as her beastly friend
jumped into the gaping hole.

"No!" Abby screamed, rushing over.

Abby threw herself over the hole. Her upper body hung into it,
looking for her mild companion. Ryan rushed over and grabbed her
arm, ensuring she wouldn't fall into the separated earth. They could
both hear eerie sounds echoing out of the opening. Nothing they
both hadn't heard before this week. There were no more growls, and
there was no sound of the beast hitting the bottom, if there even was

a bottom. Ryan pulled Abby up back on her feet and put his arm around her.

"I know it sounds stupid, but I cared about it, like it was supposed to be a part of my life. I just felt at home with them," she said, holding back tears.

Abby had spent her whole life looking for a home, and each time she got close, something had to happen. This time it was a whole new extreme, but at the same time, it was not vastly different, and the same feeling of failure and loss crept over her.

"It's not stupid," Ryan said with a smile. "In fact, you caring for a devil dog is one of the least stupid and least crazy things that I've heard this week." He continued.

Abby smiled and tried to focus at the task they were about to face. "You think it's been crazy so far. You're about to meet crazy's elder brother, the master of being fucking insane," Abby joked.

Ryan walked with Abby hand in hand until the Townsquare building was now within view. "Okay, let's go get this prick," Ryan said.

Abby admired him so much already, and now that he was willing to go running into battle with her against an unknown force, she knew she loved him an alarming amount. As they both passed a small alley, Abby pushed Ryan into it.

"What's going on?" Ryan said, confused as he was shoved against the wall. Abby held Ryan in position and looked into his eyes. "Abby?" he said, looking alarmed.

She grabbed both sides of his head and kissed him deeply. "You have to go back," she ordered.

Ryan almost looked offended at this request. "What are you talking about?" he asked. "We're stronger together," he reasoned.

"That would be true if we were up against anything else, but love weakens the hate. I need to defeat him. And if something happened to you, I would be useless," she explained.

Ryan reluctantly understood this. He wasn't stupid. In a way, he knew that if she was constantly worried about his well-being, she wouldn't be able to focus either. "As much as I don't want to leave your side, I also don't want to be the reason you get killed," he agreed.

"I love you, and I *will* be meeting you back at the car," he said as they embraced one last time before Harmon was about to change forever. As they stood there, the wind got stronger, and thunder rumbled the sky. It began to storm heavily. "This setting seems perfect for what's about to happen," Ryan said, looking down at Abby. His lips smiled, but his eyes were swept with sadness.

Abby hadn't had anyone worry about her safety ever before except Liz, of course, but she never had to deal with anything like this. It was obvious Ryan was trying to remain strong so he wouldn't be adding more to Abby's mind. They left the alley, and both looked in the opposite directions they were going in. Abby touched Ryan's arm and nudged him to start going back. She could already feel evil growing and knew it was almost time. It was no longer safe for anything that bleeds easily. Abby turned and started walking toward Townsquare.

She yelled back at Ryan, "Tell the chief to keep the police away as well unless he just wants the body count to keep growing!"

Ryan gave her the thumbs-up as they got out of yelling distance, and Abby saw him starting to dial his phone right away. *At least he heard me,* she thought.

The Townsquare building looked even worse than before. Before, it was a crime scene. Now it just looked dark and evil. Abby could sense that he was in there, but he wasn't as strong as he was before. The evil presence the hellhound made in the hospital was even stronger than this. Abby approached the building. She leaned down and pulled her boots up. Her finger ran across a rip in her jeans from when she threw herself on the broken rock to try and retrieve her friend from the opened earth it jumped into.

"And another pair bites the dust," she said to herself.

Abby went to the main doors this time, hoping Alexander would still be expecting her to sneak in. But Abby was past sneaking around. It was time to end this once and for all. As she opened the large main doors, an ax swung her way. Abby ducked with her quick reflexes and was able to dodge it entirely. She got back up and stayed low as she ducked under the doorframe and into the building, looking around for the cause of this trap. The door had been rigged to kill whoever opened it. Abby knew that if there was one trap, there were probably more. But these traps always meant there was good news. If he had to put traps up instead of posting guards, then the hospital slaughter must have taken most of Alexander's remaining men away.

"So that's why you're getting weaker," Abby whispered to herself, making the connection between why she couldn't sense his enormous amount of evil power like before and his now diminished manpower.

Abby looked around. The building was in darkness. The small amount of moonlight coming in from the windows barely helped as the storm got worse. Abby had great night vision, but the shadows were throwing her off. Abby whipped her head around as she heard movement from the other end of the room. Unlike any other normal person, Abby walked in the direction of the threat. Dealing with it now saved time instead of running away and dealing with it later. As Abby walked the length of the long main room, she noticed a stairway in the dark. She looked around and didn't see the cause of the noise. As she turned her back on the stairs, a figure jumped over the railing onto Abby, and they fell to the floor beside each other. Before she could even move, the figure jumped on top of her. It was a man, heavily tattooed with numerous scars all over his face. He put his hands around her neck and squeezed, but Abby brought her foot up and kicked him right in the side of the head. Abby got onto her knees and attempted to crawl away, but the man grabbed her leg and pulled her back. He was now holding a large knife. She grabbed it as he attempted to plunge it into her cheek. Abby struggled only for a moment before screaming as loud as she could out of intense anger. The scream sent the man across the room, where he smashed against the wall and fell like a sock monkey. Abby sat up and looked at the lifeless body lying on the ground. She wanted to feel bad because she knew that was how normal, well-adjusted people would feel about killing someone, but when she killed Alexander's men, she felt no remorse at all. Abby looked beside her at the knife that was left by the man. She picked it and tucked it into her boot. Sure, it was unlikely something so primitive would work on Alexander, but if he had any more men left, then they deserved it.

Abby got herself to her feet and decided to head for the second floor since that was where the dead guy came from. The stairs creaked as she walked up the narrow staircase. Abby held onto each side of the wall, trying to quiet her feet. The second floor was lit enough so that seeing wasn't an issue. Large candles had been lit on small edges of the walls. The wax had begun to leak down the walls onto the floor. Alexander was definitely here. Abby walked down the main hall. As she did, a gust of wind blew, not enough to blow any of the light out but enough that the flames flickered and made the setting even more unsettling for Abby. Abby stopped and looked around.

"Wind inside?" she whispered to herself.

Abby was uneasy, sure, but she wasn't experiencing fear. She carried on down the hallway until she got to another set of stairs. This time instead of looking around, she quickly walked up them. The hall was a duplicate of the second floor except it wasn't as long, and there was a door at the end of the hall instead of stairs. It appeared you couldn't continue going up from this landing. Abby went to turn back around, but the old door at the end of the hall loudly creaked open.

"That's not ominous at all," Abby said as she walked toward it.

Her attitude made her growing annoyance for Alexander's games clear. Abby walked directly to the doors. Her wedge-heeled boots clunked with every step and echoed through the building. Her presence was already known. No, her determination was too. Abby flung the doors open, and they loudly hit the walls. Small cracks grew up the walls where the trauma occurred. Abby looked around the room for any presence at all. She couldn't sense nothing and see nothing.

"Stop hiding!" she shouted. The doors slammed behind her, and Abby turned and looked. Instead of being shocked, she laughed. His tricks meant nothing to her at all. "If you're not ready for a fight with your sister, maybe you're not ready to take over an entire planet."

As she said those worlds, she could finally sense him. The room lit up fully. They were in the old town council boardroom, and Alexander was sitting on the podium, where the speaker usually stands. Alexander was dressed all in black like usual. The light glared off the spikes on the toe of his shoes. His hair was still thick with a red shimmer to it, but it was messed up unlike last time, and his eyes were visibly tired with dark circles and swelling underneath them.

"You look like you've finally had to do your own work," Abby said.

Her words echoed across the large boardroom. Alexander smiled and brushed his hair back. His smile was just as evil as his look of disdain. Alexander got up and walked slowly toward where Abby was standing. He touched everything he passed along the way, and as he touched them, the items melted down to its basic material. They didn't go up in flames and burn to ash. They just melted down. Abby watched, unimpressed with Alexander's continued tricks.

"You killed my main man," Alexander finally said. "You killed my army. You took my dogs and even gave the people of Harmon enough confidence to start hunting me. You've really laid waste to everything, Abby," Alexander said in one bland tone as he made his way toward her.

"To be fair, they were hunting you already. I just helped with their direction," Abby added.

Alexander grinned his evil grin. He was now standing directly in front of Abby. With the amount of time he took to get over there, it was although he expected her to run, but she kept her feet firmly planted. They stared at each other. Both of equal height, the similarities between them made it obvious they were related.

"Why couldn't you have just fought with me instead of against me? Think about how much stronger we would both be," Alexander explained.

"I have thought about it, and it sickens me," Abby replied.

Alexander circled Abby slowly. Abby stood still, breathing shallowly, paying attention to his every movement.

"I can sense your evil thoughts too," Alexander whispered as he got closer to Abby. "You become more transparent and predictable the more you hate me." He continued with a grin. He was still arrogant, even though he'd lost so much. "Before you try to kill me like I *know* you want to, will you at least take a walk with me and let me show you some things?" Alexander asked. Abby looked at him, puzzled. "All you have to do is look and listen. Then if you wish to war, so be it," he requested.

She knew that he was stalling and not as strong as he was. He didn't want the war he was acting so calm about. Abby stared at Alexander with disgust and shared his evil grin.

"Sure, I'll play," she said, waiting to see what desperate action he would try next.

Chapter 16

A bby stood bold and prepared in place. She motioned for Alexander to open the door and start the field trip he requested. She could feel him inside her head watching her thoughts like a sitcom.

"You can try to block me out, but everyone thinks of their desires eventually," Alexander said as he walked through the doors that sprung open without being touched.

Abby didn't answer since this wasn't the only tour she was beginning. She was also attended a tour within Alexander's head. While he was shuffling around in Abby's mess of a mind, he was unaware that Abby was already deep inside his head, planting thoughts and images of her own. Alexander walked straight for the stairs at the end of the hall but kept going when he got to the top as if in his mind, the hallway was still going. He tumbled down the stairs, violently hitting a wall at the bottom of the next floor. As he smacked his head against the wall, Abby was finally alone in her own head. He yelled, not in pain but in anger, and the whole building shook. Abby walked down to Alexander, who was literally fuming mad with his hair glowing and flaming. Abby walked right up to him, sparing no space.

"And stay out," she said abrasively, referring to his intrusion into her mind.

Alexander's breathing slowed down, and his body started to resemble a regular human again. "Don't pull that shit again!" he yelled.

"Don't give me a reason to!" Abby snapped back.

Alexander wiped his face with both hands and turned to keep walking. He looked visibly flustered now and clearly didn't know how powerful his sister had become. Abby followed. Alexander got to the main floor and headed to the back of the building. He opened the door, and yellow caution fell and blew in the wind. The storm had stopped, but the sky remained darkened with clouds. They stepped outside into the familiar area. The glass was still scattered around the pool, where Abby had jumped from the building to safety the first time she had met Alexander. Now here they were, in the same place together and alone, something Abby never thought would happen.

"This way," Alexander said gruffly as he headed to the tunnel Abby had spent far too much time in already.

"We're going back into the tunnels? They're guarded," Abby replied.

"We're going deeper," Alexander replied.

Abby remembered the heat and insane things that happened in those tunnels last time as she followed Alexander into what she thought might be her last moment alive. Abby knew one thing. If he was leading her to death, then she was taking him down with her. Abby watched Alexander climb onto the ladder and disappear into the darkness first. She waited for a moment and then followed down as well. She got to the bottom and jumped from the ladder. Her boots splashed to disgusting liquid mixture up Alexander's pants. He looked down at his pants and grunted.

"That's one thing I actually didn't mean to do," Abby said with a small giggle.

"I'm sure," he said with sarcasm leaking from his mouth.

The opening of the tunnel that Abby knew led to the river was visible from where they were standing. Not greatly, but a small amount of moonlight could be seen showing the opening. Two guards were still there, but Abby and Alexander had gone unnoticed.

"Let's go," Alexander said as he began to walk further into the tunnels the way Abby and Ryan had went.

They got to the end of the tunnel, and Alexander lifted the slab of concrete with ease that Ryan had issues with. He threw it against the wall, and it smashed.

"Well, that's not going to attract the guards," Abby said sarcastically.

"Just get down here," Alexander said as he just jumped into the hole legs first.

Abby took the normal way down and used the ladder. When she got to the bottom, it was much different than she remembered. The bloodbath was gone. All the bodies had been cleaned up, and the creepy art that messed with Ryan was gone as well. All that was left were dark red bloodstains that had also been faded out from the vigorous scrubbing the whole place seemed to have gotten. Alexander didn't keep going into the tunnels or the area where they had rescued Cassie from. He instead lifted one of the undamaged statues that Abby had judged upon noticing last time. Underneath was another small hatch. He pulled it, and it opened. Lots of light shone through the door. He climbed in without words, assuming Abby would follow, which she did out of mere curiosity. She closed the hatch and covered it as good as she could before descending. It wasn't a far drop this time. It was only about ten steps. In fact, it was so close that when Abby was looking around, she could hear the footsteps of an officer searching the tunnel above for them.

One officer could be heard yelling, "Do you see anything?"

To which the other one responded, "No, probably just some dumb kids."

Then the steps could be heard shuffling around more. The clanging of their work boots against the metal ladder echoed as they went back up to the surface.

A tiny room at the end of the ladder led to an ajar door. The last thing Abby wanted to do was compliment Alexander, but this place was gorgeous. Inside, the walls were red, and the floors were black marble. It wasn't a whole tunnel like the floors above, but the room was about the size of a medium-sized gymnasium anyway.

"I can tell you feel at home here," Alexander said as he watched his sister's expressions.

"When you die, I'm moving here," Abby said. This set Alexander back for a moment. "Did you think that taking me for a walk and showing me a pretty room would change my mind?" Abby laughed.

Alexander laughed with her. At least Abby hoped it was with her. "You misunderstand. This place is already yours," Alexander said, pointing around the room. Abby followed his finger pointing around the room and observed. It was totally her style, and she did feel at home there. "All you have to do is stop destroying my empire and start helping me build it," he explained.

"That's why you sent that giant freak to take me. When I woke up, those weird women were preparing me to come down here, weren't they?" Abby accused.

Alexander smiled at her as she connected events. "You would have woken up feeling at peace here at home. With family," Alexander said.

This was something Abby had always dreamed of, not only to have a family but also for them to actually want her and have a place for her. But there was only one problem. Abby's brother didn't want her; he *needed* her and wouldn't hesitate to kill her if she wasn't of use to him. Abby knew this, which was why she never turned her back on Alexander once.

"A week ago, that may have actually worked," Abby said. "But not now," she concluded.

Abby had spent her whole life looking for a place she belonged, only to find out that the place where she belonged wasn't at all where she wanted to be. She wanted to be where she didn't belong now, with Ryan and the rest of the police force taking down people who were just as evil as her.

"I told you to stay out!" Abby yelled as she felt Alexander step inside her head again. *Since you're in here, two can play at that game,* Abby thought, knowing Alexander would be able to hear. Abby let her mind go blank as she entered into Alexander's. "So that's why you needed the girls," she said with disappointment in her voice.

"Wouldn't you eat a few pure organs of a virgin nobody to live forever?" Alexander said with a sinister look.

Abby looked at him with disgust. Not only is cannibalism weird and disgusting, but also living forever just sounded exhausting. "No wonder you're moody. We took your food away before you were finished," Abby said mockingly.

"You joke, but you caused a huge blow. Between taking my men and my sustenance away, you've made me very desperate," Alexander replied. "That can be either good or extremely bad for you." He continued in a threatening manner.

"I agree, desperation is one of the best motivators. That's exactly how the Harmon police felt. Desperate. And for that, I thank you. Through that desperation, they were forced to trust me and, in doing so, giving me a place somewhere," Abby said to Alexander, who looked puzzled at her words.

Alexander walked the length of the room, while Abby stood in place, staring at him. One of his last remaining men carefully came through the door. The look of terror on his face when he had to step through the door into the same room as the siblings was one that Abby wouldn't soon forget. This man's thoughts weren't evil at all, maybe at one point but not now. Memories of the men he grew close to dying at the hospital while he and a handful of other men escaped riddled his mind. A woman burning, her screams to him as he reached for her. Then an explosion. This man had been through hell and was still forced to serve his evil boss. He held a tray that kept shaking in his grasp.

"Set it down and get out, Stephen," Alexander commanded.

"Stephen, why do you stay here?" Abby asked as the man walked toward the door on his boss's order.

"I do not want to burn, ma'am," Stephen said with a slight accent that sounded German. He looked at her for only a split second and then put his head back down and exited the room as if he had done something wrong.

"You really know how to treat your employees," Abby snapped.

"He knows he's here for my benefit. Now eat," Alexander said, pointing to the tray his abused soldier brought in.

Chapter 17

Alexander uncovered the tray. It actually looked great—steak, potatoes, corn. At least it looked like steak.

"I don't eat people or wish to live any longer than I have to," Abby said, looking away from the dish.

Alexander fixed himself a plate and sat. "It's cow. Don't tell you're vegetarian? These ordinary humans are really rubbing off on you." Alexander laughed. Abby watched him cut what looked like normal meat and put it in his mouth. It was so rare that blood ran down Alexander's chin as he chewed. "Not as good as what I actually need, but I'll rectify that soon enough," Alexander said with the half-eaten cow still slopping around in his mouth.

"I wasn't a vegetarian before, but after witnessing this, I might be," Abby said in disgust as she sat in a red chair directly across from the matching one he was sitting in. Was this his last meal? Or was Alexander offering Abby her last meal? Alexander ate like an animal. Food fell out of his mouth and onto the floor. A small piece of meat rolled across the floor and touched Abby's boot, leaving a small amount of blood from the barely cooked meat. "Really?" Abby said as she leaned over and grabbed the napkin from Alexander's plate to wipe her boot. "Because they haven't been covered with enough blood lately?" she snapped sarcastically as she threw herself back down in her chair.

Alexander smirked as he finished eating. He slammed his plate down so hard that without words, his man Stephen came running into the room to clear the dirty dish away. Abby looked at Stephen and him at her. His only evil thoughts were now also about Alexander, but Alexander was too busy trying to surf around inside Abby's head, and with his now limited power, he didn't seem to want to overextend it. Stephen left the room safe. His wish for Alexander's death remained a secret between him and Abby.

"There's more," Alexander said as he walked on, expecting Abby to follow. Abby did follow, not by direction but to merely satisfy her curiosity.

The more they walked into the giant room, the larger it seemed to get. In the far corner, there was a huge king bed. Plush red blankets hung off it, and a red canopy gently covered it. There was a decorative fireplace next to it and a robe. Abby walked over to the bedroom area within the open concept layer. Written across the black robe in red was the name Abigail Briggs. Abby traced the name with her index finger until she noticed Alexander standing right behind her.

"You weren't joking about this being my place, were you?" Abby stated in the form of a question.

"I told you that you belong with the family," Alexander said roughly.

Abby spun around to reply, but as she turned, something caught her eye. Her face went even whiter than her normal pale tone. Abby pushed Alexander to the side as she walked by him.

"What the hell is this doing here?" Abby said with both fear and anger in her voice. It was the same huge painting from the hall upstairs that somehow was able to move and entangle Ryan. "I thought this was destroyed," Abby said. Abby stood in front of it and examined it from a distance. The red-and-black strokes of the paint just made a mess, not a picture.

Alexander walked over very slowly as he spoke. "It can't be destroyed," he said.

Abby looked back at Alexander like he was a total moron. "Anything can be destroyed if you try hard enough," she said with a veiled threat.

Alexander smiled. "It's a portrait of our father," he said as he walked up to it and ran his hand across the middle portion.

"Really? Our father is a bunch of pointless lines and slashes of paint?" Abby said, making it more than obvious that her patience was wearing thin.

"No, no," Alexander said with a loud laugh that echoed through the structure, giving her an uneasy feeling. "The human mind can't comprehend the amount of evil in one painting," Alexander explained.

"You really expect me to believe *you* are human?" Abby questioned.

"Half. I'm exactly as you are," Alexander replied.

Abby gave him a foul look. "Exactly like me? Now you're just being insulting," Abby hissed.

Alexander still laughed at her sarcasm. "Once we die, we'll be able to see him for what he truly is. Until then, the image of our father would just cause madness to the human portion of our minds." Alexander continued to explain.

"So it's our brains jumbling the image, not him?" Abby asked. She couldn't believe she was actually having a conversation with Alexander. She was actually letting him speak to her instead of just killing him right then and there. He admitted himself that he was weakened now.

"If you're asking if he's present or if he was the one who attacked your little boyfriend with the paint strokes, then the answer is no. That was all me," Alexander said, claiming his actions. "I actually feel as though he likes you more than me," Alexander said.

Abby wasn't sure why he would even say that. "What could possibly make you think that?" Abby said with pure confusion.

"Because I'm creating too much attention now. He won't even speak to me anymore, but you have the nerve to block him out," Alexander said as though he was offended.

"I'm an orphan. I have no interest in either one of my parents, so if this is childish jealousy, then you can put the brakes on it," Abby said. "I still want that out of here."

Alexander nodded to her words and shouted at Stephen to come in. Stephen came running in with haste right away since he seemed like he was posted just outside the door. Alexander pointed at the painting. "Take this upstairs," he ordered.

"But, sir, I—" Stephen said before getting cut off.

"Now!" Alexander shouted, causing a crack in a glass mirror that Abby hadn't even noticed by the bed.

Stephen grabbed the painting, and Abby turned away. She looked back to see him struggling to drag it out of the room but with determination on his face.

Alexander headed for a very small door beside the sitting area. Abby looked to him after she watched the creepy painting leave the area. "Am I following you?" she shouted at Alexander.

Without words, he beckoned at her to come. Alexander had to duck through the door, and as Abby followed, she almost hit her head as she didn't duck far enough since she was the same height as her brother. The tiny door led to a very darkened area.

"Um, hello?" Abby said as she walked in.

Part of her was trying to prepare herself in case this was a trick. An explosive buzzing noise deafened Abby for a moment until her ears adjusted. Her eyes also had to take a moment as Alexander had flipped a power switch, and aged overhead lights flickered as they began to come to life. Abby looked around. The room had recently been cleaned. The tiled floors were shining as though they had just been scrubbed. The walls had shelves and shelves of books and historical objects, all very familiar items.

"All this stuff is from the Harmon Library," Abby said with shock. She grabbed at some of the books and flipped through them. They were all stamped with the library's address and name. "Why would you burn down a building but keep its contents?" Abby asked, trying to piece things together.

"I thought you would be happy that I didn't burn the city's history with the building," Alexander said. Now his voice was coated with confusion. "Isn't what I'm doing to the city the reason for your hatred toward me?" Alexander asked.

Abby dropped the books that she was holding and began laughing, not a soft giggle but a full laugh as though Alexander had just told her the funniest joke she had ever heard. "You think I want to kill you because of the terror you caused upon the city?" Abby laughed.

Alexander looked at her with a blank look on his face, clearly unable to decide how to react. "For once, I'm afraid I don't understand," Alexander blandly said.

Abby was caught between blind answer and hysterical amusement. How could someone so powerful be so clueless? Abby paced for a moment to calm down. It wasn't time to fight yet. "You think I've been putting all this effort into finding you for Harmon? A city that's never been kind to me. I owe it nothing," Abby said.

Alexander looked around the room at his wasted efforts to please his sister. "Then why? Why have you gone out of your way to cause me problems?" he demanded to know.

"Are you serious?" Abby said as she got closer to Alexander. She looked into his face, unable to believe that he could know so much yet so little. "Your men killed my boss, my only friend, Liz. Then they burned down my place of employment. You also sent a giant freak to kidnap me. Then you sent him back to kill me and someone I adore in the hospital," Abby said, trying to pick the worst of the incidents as there were far too many to choose from. "Is that enough, or should I keep going?" Abby said snidely.

"So this isn't about the city?" Alexander said, still confused.

Abby's anger was starting to get out of control. "The cops care about what you're doing to the city. For me, this is personal. You made it personal," Abby hissed. She turned around and went to leave the small makeshift library, but the door slammed shut. "This isn't time for games," Abby said.

"We're not done here," Alexander commanded her like he did with his men.

Abby kicked the door, and it flew across the room and shattered the already cracked mirror beside the sleeping area. "That's a shame. I liked that mirror," she said to herself.

Alexander followed her back out into her room or prison cell if you believe in free will. "I can honestly say I don't know who Liz is," Alexander said, hoping it would calm her down and make himself appear innocent in this one situation.

It didn't calm Abby down; in fact, it had the opposite effect. Abby was getting so angry that her long red hair was once again starting to flame, and the color of her eyes was on the edge of changing to their angry red hue. Alexander put his hand out to motion for her to stop for a moment.

"The men that did it are dead now, right? Isn't that enough justice?" Alexander asked or pleaded.

Abby grinned a far more evil grin that Alexander had ever shown. Her eyes calmed down, but her hair remained alive with fire. "Justice. Justice," Abby repeated over and over to herself. "That just doesn't sound right coming out of your mouth." Abby laughed.

Alexander looked on at Abby. Even though it was his sister, she was beautiful. Her eyes shone from the flames that danced along each strand of her hair. She was the most elegant display of evil he had ever seen. She was also much more powerful and emotionally driven than Alexander was expected.

"And what would justice be right now?" Alexander asked Abby as she stared deeply at him. The positions of the siblings had shifted so much since their first encounter.

"Justice to me or in general? Because those are two very different outcomes," Abby replied.

Alexander sat in one of the matching red chairs facing Abby. "How so?" Alexander asked.

"Justice for everyone would be a trial for all your crimes so everyone gets closure. My kind of justice would be a quick execution right away to just get rid of the problem," Abby said without remorse.

Abby sat in the chair across from Alexander. Once again, they were facing each other. They remained silent while they thought about the two options Abby listed. Alexander broke the silence.

"A trial might be fun. I like knowing I have an effect on people," Alexander said.

"You're trying to push me in the other direction because you think you'll win a big brawl with me." Abby laughed.

Alexander joined the laugh. "I can either win the fight with you here or go be entertained on trial and leave my cell whenever I choose. I don't dislike these options," he mocked.

"I'd see to it that you wouldn't escape," Abby said with a more serious tone.

Alexander kept laughing. "I'm sure you would try with all your might." He laughed.

"Let's walk up to the surface then. If you're not worried about what might happen, then let's go," Abby said as she walked over and opened the door.

Stephen was standing right outside it and looked in as she opened it.

"Get out!" Alexander screamed, causing the whole place to shake.

Abby wondered if the people above felt it and thought it was a small earthquake. Stephen's footsteps got heavier the more he ran until he had climbed to the next level and it was silent outside the door. Alexander got up and followed, to Abby's surprise. Although he saw her as his biggest threat now, he still carried himself in this situation with amusement instead of remorse or fear. Abby climbed to the top and continued going until she got to the top level. She was met by police officers. Alexander's remaining man, Stephen, was on the ground in cuffs. The officer drew their weapons and demanded Abby to get on the ground. Abby held her finger up, signaling them to give her a moment. The officers reacted as though this was a sign of disrespect and tried to grab Abby. As they went to touch her arm, her body gave out a high level of hot energy that sent them flying and hitting the side of the tunnel like a small explosion. The officers landed on the tunnel floor uninjured. They got up and ran, forgetting their prisoner. Abby was already on edge and angry, which meant she was fuming hot. She walked over to Stephen. He flinched in fear as she reached to touch him. Without seconds of her touching his cuffs, they were melted into a liquid metal.

"Run, and find me after this is over if you want a cleaner job," Abby said as she pointed to the tunnel opening where the officers had already fled.

Abby waited. A part of her expected Alexander to disappear within the tunnels again, but she hoped that wouldn't happen and every person he affected could finally get some closure. A moment later, Alexander's head popped up from the opening. The thought of him getting to be able to sit in a courtroom and listen to all the hurt he had brought on to the public was too much for him to turn down. Alexander got up and stood beside her.

"Now what? You scared off the cops you were going to turn me in to," Alexander joked.

"That's not the cop that will be bringing you in," Abby said.

She started walking toward the opening of the tunnel. Light shone through where the bars used to be. They had been removed once the area became a crime scene. It was morning. She had spent most of the night with Alexander. She walked to the tunnel opening and carefully climbed down the sides as not to end up in the river again. Alexander jumped from the opening of the tunnel to the grass, a distance no ordinary human would have ever attempted, and he actually made it. Abby climbed down onto the grass. It was still wet from the snow that had melted, but at this point, Abby wasn't sure if that was a couple of days ago or a week ago. She just wasn't to get some kind of normal back to her life. It would never be normal by any normal person's terms, but normal to her would be fine. Abby walked toward Townsquare so they could get to the other side, where she was going to meet Ryan.

She kept looking at her brother walking beside her. She had never seen him in daylight before. They looked so much alike. Their skin tone was the same identical pale shade. Her hair was a much richer red, but the red hue to his matched her as well. She dressed in a black leather jacket with black thigh-high boots that covered her aged jeans. Alexander dressed also in a black leather jacket, though his was almost floor length, and he also had black boots on, though his had spikes pointing out on each side. They looked like siblings even to an untrained eye. With how pale his skin was, it was easy to see the darkness around his eyes. Paired with his heavy breathing, it was made clear that he wasn't finished getting sustenance from Cassie, and it was making him weak. This alone was the reason she was okay with him breathing the same air as Ryan. Alexander wouldn't waste his remaining energy on one single person.

Alexander looked around as they exited Townsquare. The splits in the earth that Abby and Ryan had encountered were still there, but they were no longer steaming or harboring strange noises within them. Alexander smiled at his destruction.

"So what makes you think no one will try and kill me in jail? I'm sure I've killed more cops' families than just your little lover's," he said, edging Abby into further anger.

"You said before you can escape, so I'm sure you can take care of your own physical threats," Abby said, trying to remain calm.

"You just don't seem like the type that would like the death of their own brother on their conscience," he said, trying to dig at Abby's head now that Ryan's car was in view.

But it wasn't just Ryan. Chief Doyle stood in the distance, along with a large amount of the Harmon police force. The two officers who fled from the tunnel must have radioed in, and they pieced together what was happening.

Abby looked at their welcoming party and then replied to Alexander's remark, "I may not have killed you but just know that I was prepared to. And I would have slept like a baby with a clear conscience tonight."

Abby tried to walk on before she was grabbed by the arm by Alexander in an aggressive way. Much like the officers in the tunnel, Alexander was thrown from Abby with intense force. He was thrown away from her at incredible speed. It just looked like a streak of fire in the sky. Alexander's engulfed limp body crashed against the side of a building closer to the line of officers. His body dropped to the ground. He looked like a fireball until the flames went out to reveal Alexander flustered but unharmed. Bricks from the now damaged building fell beside where Alexander lay. Abby rushed over to him, jumping over the cracks in the road. She grabbed Alexander by the back of the neck with such force that she lifted him to her feet.

"Do *not* do that again. It hurts me too," she said in a rough voice.

Alexander smiled his evil smile. There was a small amount of blood in his mouth that he spit as they walked toward the cops. She did injure him nominally. As she approached, she noticed Ryan walking toward her. He walked his haste but also with caution. The look on all the officers' faces as they saw the most dangerous man in the world as they knew it approach them was unreadable. Fear, satisfaction, anger—they were overwhelmed. Chief Doyle walked behind Ryan.

"Abby," Ryan said as he stood in front of them.

"He surrenders," Abby said, handing him off to the chief.

Multiple officers surrounded Alexander with their guns drawn. Ryan and Abby looked on as they tied Alexander's hands.

"Will that even work?" Ryan asked Abby.

Abby looked at Ryan, so happy to just hear his voice again. "It'll work for as long as he wants it to," Abby replied.

Ryan wanted to wait until they were alone but couldn't wait any longer and wrapped his arms around Abby tightly. "You have to tell me everything," he said, looking at her.

"I can just show you once I know he'll be secure," Abby replied loud enough for Chief Doyle to overhear.

The chief walked over to calm her worries about that. "Alexander will be tied up with a flame-resistant material, and he'll have a whole unit of officers with guns drawn on him at all times. He'll be here when you get back," Chief Doyle said. "You two," the chief said, pointing at two uniformed officers, "go with Detective Finney and document what you need to."

The two officers followed Abby and Ryan back to Townsquare. "It's at the back of the Townsquare building, the same tunnel opening we went into before," she said as she started running toward the building. She ran around the building and through the grounds, not even noticing the pool where she almost lost her life. Small amounts of mud and water were kicked up by Abby's boots as she ran across the open grass to the opening. "It's all the way back down here, but we missed it because it was deeper," she said, rushing into the tunnel.

"Why are you rushing so much?" Ryan asked as him, and the other two officers caught up.

"I don't trust leaving Alexander alone too long," Abby said as she jumped off the metal ladder and onto the ground.

"He's surrounded by very capable officers," Ryan said without enough enthusiasm in that comment to even convince himself.

Ryan struggled to find his footing at the bottom of the ladder. Abby grabbed him around the waist and helped him down.

"I don't mean to insult your men, but they are just that, men. And you've lost enough of them to Alexander to know that if something can bleed, he can kill it," Abby said, trying to be nice as possible.

Ryan stared at Abby for a moment. Her hair was brighter, and so were her eyes. The more powerful she got, the more her appearance changed to fit what she was absorbing. "You look beautiful," he said. "Scarily beautiful."

Ryan leaned in, about to place his lips on Abby's, when one of the officers escorting them jumped from the ladder into the tunnel. They were quickly snapped back into reality, and Abby started walking in the direction she came from.

"This way," she said.

The officers were both in the tunnel now and followed behind Ryan. As they approached the opening in the floor, one of the officers got uneasy. He was one of the officers who stormed the tunnels before and found the dozens of bodies from Alexander's personal prison.

"It's all cleaned up, if that makes everyone feel better," Abby said.

When they got closer to the opening, Ryan looked over at the slab of concrete that he could barely lift. "Did you do that?" he said, pointing at it smashed by the wall.

"Alexander," she replied as she dropped without hesitation into the hole.

Ryan quickly followed as Abby only had to wait for a couple of seconds for him to join her. Ryan went to walk through the tunnels.

"There's no need," she said. "It's right here," she said, pointing to a partly rolled-up rug.

She moved it to reveal an opening that was still unlatched. Abby went to drop herself down another hole again but was stopped by Ryan.

"Let them go first," he requested.

"But I was just there," she said, confused.

But the officers followed their superior officer's order and climbed down. Ryan and Abby waited for a moment, listening for any indication of what was happening down there. Only moments later, one of the officers yelled, "All clear," up at them.

Ryan waited for Abby and helped her down so she wouldn't have to jump yet again. The small room at the bottom of the stairs was lit by the light from the open door leading to the room that was meant for Abby. When they walked in, it looked the same, and once again, Abby wanted to live there.

"Wow," Ryan said. "I was expecting it to be ugly and gory like Alexander, but this is beautiful." He continued as he walked around the large room, looking at the decor. He came across the same robe as Abby did with her name branded across it. "So is this why he brought you here?" Ryan asked, looking at Abby while he displayed the robe to her in his hand.

"Yes and no," Abby replied, pointing to the small door near the chairs.

Ryan walked over and let himself in. The brightness of the old lighting took him a moment, but he recognized the library items right away. "I need you two to start taking the stuff in this room up to the surface," Ryan ordered the officers. "And treat it like evidence," Ryan added. It was not like they needed any more evidence to take Alexander down, but Ryan was very thorough.

"I want to live here," Abby said, to the surprise of the two officers walking past her with their arms full of evidence.

"Why?" Ryan said, looking around.

Abby walked toward the large bed and threw herself on it. "I can't explain it. I've just never felt so at home," she answered as she sunk into the comfort of the massive king bed.

"Well, I'm sure once we've gathered evidence, we can make a request to Chief Doyle. You've done enough to deserve it," Ryan said.

Abby felt a small amount of excitement run through her body. "We should head back up to the surface before I head too cozy," Abby joked.

Ryan took ahold of Abby's hand mindlessly, and they walked to the door. Abby went up first on each ladder with Ryan placing his hands on her thighs for support.

On the surface, most of the officers, including the chief, had already left with Alexander, leaving behind a handful of officers to assist Ryan and collect evidence for the trial Alexander was looking forward to being amused by.

"Am I being paranoid, or should I be this worried about the evil fuck escaping?" Ryan said with a language that turned Abby on a bit.

"Are they still at the hospital?" Abby asked.

"No, we've set up a temporary station at the old headquarters so we aren't interfering with patient care while conducting police business," he replied. "It's a very outdated facility," he added, expressing his concern once more.

"Let's head there," Abby suggested.

Ryan looked concerned about bringing Abby there but knew that they had already brought the biggest threat in already. "All right, but I doubt you'll be able to get in and see him," he mentioned, and they both walked back to his car. It was still parked in the same position it was in before they parted before.

"Thank you for waiting for me," Abby said softly as she realized he hadn't left his spot for many hours.

"Always," Ryan replied with a smile.

They both got in the car, and Ryan began to drive to the new/old station. Abby held Ryan's hand the whole way there. They barely talked, but an overwhelming calm was coming over her. Alexander was finally weak enough to answer to his unspeakable crimes, and Abby was loved. Her only wish was that Liz was still alive to see it.

After all, she was the one who told her to never give up on finding happiness.

The station was made from pure brick. It was obvious why the basic structure of the building withstood all the abuse the city had taken. The building was unmarked, but the amount of police vehicle surrounded it made it clear what it was used for. There were two armed police officers guarding the front entrance as they walked in. Abby looked at them as she passed. One of the officers nodded to Ryan in recognition as they allowed them both to pass. As they entered, the stress on the officers' faces was so obvious.

"There you two are!" yelled Chief Doyle as he walked out of a small office across the tiny room where many officers were bunched together working.

"I figured you might be expecting both of us," Ryan answered as they met just outside the chief's door and shook hands.

"Of course, you two are quite the buzz around here," the chief said as the other officers looked up and started whispering, unaware that they couldn't hide their thoughts from Abby, let alone their whispers. Some of the officers weren't happy that their chief was trusting a relative of Alexander, but most of the officers were grateful for what Abby and Ryan had done. "These last seven hours while Alexander was distracted with Abby and after he was brought in have been the calmest hours our police force has seen in many years," Chief Doyle said to Ryan.

Ryan walked around the tiny station with the chief by his side, while Abby listened from a distance. "Where is he being held?" Ryan asked.

Chief Doyle pointed to a darkened door with large prints that said, "Authorized Personnel Only." "There's some concern over how heavy the guard should be and what should happen if he were to attempt an escape," the chief said, looking back at Abby.

Abby walked over to accept the invitation into the conversation. "I can help, I think," Abby offered.

Ryan interjected, "You've given Alexander enough of your time."

Abby laughed. "That's not what I meant," she said. "Can I see him?" she asked.

All officers within ear reach turned and looked at her. The chief shared their stare for a moment. "None of my officers will even tend to this prisoner's care, but you want to visit him?" Chief Doyle asked, making sure he heard Abby's request right.

"It's not like I'm bringing him tea. I just need to know how secure he is," Abby explained.

Ryan looked at the chief and shrugged, unwilling to be put in between the two most powerful and influential people in his life. "She hasn't steered us wrong before, sir, only helped us," he added, hoping to help Abby's case. Abby looked to the chief before moving toward the door.

"Fine, I'll give you three minutes with the nutcase," Chief Doyle said roughly.

Abby walked to the door, and before she opened it, Ryan placed his hand on it. "We'll be right outside if you need anything," he said, still trying to be the brave boyfriend, even though he knew how powerful his girlfriend was at this point.

Abby touched his hand and leaned over to him. She kissed him on the cheek, not caring that the chief was watching. "I'll be fine," she said as she gently moved Ryan's hand out of the way and opened the door.

Abby walked into the jail and closed the door behind her. The cells were completely empty except for one way down at the end in a corner cell. Alexander sat cross-legged on the floor in what looked to be a meditative state. Abby walked over to the cell and spoke, interrupting his process.

"I still don't understand what your plan is," she said. Alexander didn't answer but opened his eyes and smiled widely at the sight of his sister standing before him. "You're in a jail cell, pretty much all your men are dead, and yet you still seem to have hope. That makes me believe there's a plan," Abby reasoned as she slid down the bar to the cell across from Alexander and sat on the ground.

"Actions are all about timing," Alexander said softly as he closed his eyes again and relaxed his shoulders.

Abby sat there looking at him for a moment. "So you want me to believe that the most powerful man in Harmon is going to sit in a cell, waiting for the right timing to escape?" Abby said to Alexander without a reply.

She attempted to see what he was planning, but his constant state of deep meditation was protecting his mind from her snooping around. Abby could see that there was no reasoning with Alexander right now. Instead, she closed her eyes as well and focused. Her palms were placed on the ground beneath her as she pictured her loyal companions. It took seconds for screams to erupt from the station, screams of shock, not terror. When Abby opened her eyes, she could see the shadows of Ryan and Chief Doyle moving away from the doors quickly. Ryan's hand reached over the door, and Abby's faithful beasts walked into the jail. The door flung open from the hellhounds' sizes, and Alexander was more alert as he heard the noises of what were once his pets. Four of the beasts were now sitting around the spot where Abby was on the floor. Ryan and the chief looked on through the open door. The other officers in the station were all crowded at the door, trying to see in as well. Abby got up and spoke to the confused Alexander once the hounds had settled.

"Since you're acting like an escape is possible, my friends will be keeping an eye on you. I think we both know what they'll do to you if you step foot outside this cell," Abby said, threatening the once powerful man.

Alexander looked around, stumped. He may have been able to defend himself against the turned hellhounds before, but now that he had lost a lot of himself, he was almost fully mortal now. Even he knew that being eaten alive by a hellhound was the worst death he could think of. Abby petted one of the growling creatures on its head as she left the jail, closing the door partly. When she got out into the mail portion of the station, every cop in there was staring at her. The thoughts in their heads ranged anywhere from calling her a freak to pure amazement by the new animals. The cops who were at the hospital were actually smiling with contentment to see the hounds again.

"Will they be staying here?" Chief Doyle asked, breaking the uncomfortable silence.

"Until I call them away," Abby replied.

Ryan put his hands on both their shoulders. "Maybe it's best if we go talk in your office, sir," he suggested as he was already trying to walk them in that direction.

The chief followed Ryan's direction without words. Still unused to the things that had been occurring, he was frozen and unsure of what to do next. Chief Doyle looked back to see the officers going in and out of the jail, totally over their fear of Alexander. In fact, they were paying no attention to him but kept running back and forth, feeding the hounds scraps of their lunches from a small aged fridge against the wall. These were unlike any other K9s that the officers were used to, but the officers enjoyed having them there regardless.

Abby and Ryan sat in the two uncomfortable plastic chairs facing the chief's desk. Chief Doyle sat on a squeaky old computer chair and paused for a moment.

"Okay, the transportation of Alexander to the courthouse, will these creatures listen to us, or should we have you present?" Chief Doyle said, looking in Abby's direction.

"They will guard him no matter what, I believe, but I would like to be here in case anything goes wrong," Abby said.

Chief Doyle nodded at her request and looked to Ryan. "There's some things I need to discuss with Detective Finney alone before I can confirm anything. There's coffee and hot chocolate on top of the fridge," he said, pointing to the small fridge that the officers were still searching through, hoping to find more things to feed the hounds.

Ryan spoke up. "She's okay to stay, sir. I—"

Abby cut him off. "It's okay," she said as she got up out of the awful chair.

She put her hand on his arm as she turned and left the little office, closing the door behind her out of respect for their privacy. As soon as she closed the door, all the cops looked up at her again. Their curiosity about her made her uneasy. She was just hoping none of them would get too familiar and start asking questions, questions that she was just learning the answers to. Instead, she stepped outside and took in some air.

Now that the hellhounds were taking care of the security threat within the police station, the two armed guards at the front had been told they could stand down. Abby was actually alone for a moment. It was such an odd feeling. After spending the last twenty years alone, she had spent over a week barely alone at all. It was starting to get draining. She decided to go for a walk around the block. It was daylight, so there were some people out and about. It was weird for her to see regular people going on with their daily lives, unaware of what just happened, that within one night, their city was so much safer than it was before. Of course, Abby knew what the police would be worried about. When a large crime boss gets taken down, someone always tries to take their place. It wouldn't be the end of their problems, but it was the end of the problems that they couldn't solve themselves. Now regular gangsters and criminals could take over the streets again. At least bullets worked on them, and they would live above ground. Abby was so focused on getting to Alexander and making sure he was actually in a cell that she actually had no idea what part of Harmon they were in. It seemed like the outskirts of the city. There used to be a station that would catch speeders heading into the city from the main highway, but once speeding became that least of their problems, they only operated from the central station. Abby figured out that this must be that same old station that was closed over fifteen years ago. She walked until she found the highway and confirmed this theory. The highway shared a story of its own. The tire tracks of people leaving the city, skidding along the way, were very clear, but the lane coming into the city had grass growing over it. Harmon's reputation made everyone stay away and turned it into a dying town. Abby felt slightly proud that they may have not only just saved all of Alexander's future victims but that they also probably saved the whole city of Harmon.

Chapter 18

The streets of Harmon were the calmest they had been in years. Alexander was stashed away in a cell while Abby's unkillable beasts guarded him. Abby walked back the way she came from and saw the new/old police station in her view. Ryan was out on the front steps, looking around presumably for Abby. She waved, and he walked down the steps in her direction. Though his arm was on the fast-track to healing the stress it had suffered, these last few days had torn some of the already dissolving stitches. Abby noticed Ryan had some new bandaging on. She spoke to him once he got within ear range.

"Are you okay?" Abby said, touching Ryan's arm.

"I will be," he said with a smile. "The dogs are guarding him, and he's not moving. The chief told us to take the rest of the day to rest," Ryan said.

"Should we really do that?" Abby said, thinking of all the ways things could go wrong if they weren't there.

"Maybe we shouldn't, but we have to. We're only human, or at least I am," Ryan replied.

Abby smiled gently and walked toward his car. Ryan got in the driver's side. He wasn't acting like his arm was hurting him, but maybe that was just a brave face. They drove back to the apartment building, but that wasn't home for Abby anymore. She already knew where she wanted to live. When they pulled in the back parking lot, Abby started to feel her eyes get heavy. Even for her, sleep was a necessity, an annoyance but required. Abby hated driving up to her building now. The empty lot where Duffy's bar once was just left her with the memories of the day Liz was killed. Whenever she thought about it, she started second-guessing her choice to bring Alexander in to answer for his crimes instead of killing him. He deserved whatever happened to him and more.

They walked into the building, and Abby went to go to her apartment, while Ryan went toward his. He grabbed her by the hand and guided her into his place instead. Ryan's place looked exactly the same, but you could tell he hadn't been there in a long time. As soon as Ryan got into his place, he locked his door and dead bolted it. He kicked his pants off and carefully lifted his shirt over his head. Abby watched while she walked into his bedroom. Once in there, she got completely naked and slipped under the covers, facing away from the other side of the bed. Ryan walked in still wearing his boxers. Abby was totally exhausted, but the budge in his underwear made her stare.

"Do you need anything?" Ryan said as he slipped off his boxers.

His boxers joined the floor with all of Abby's clothing. Ryan looked at the pile of her clothes and back at her. His resting manhood was now perking up once he realized he had a naked redhead in his bed. His package bounced as he walked across the room out of Abby's view and got into bed behind her. He snuggled up to her from behind and wrapped his arms around her. Ryan had swelled up completely now. Abby could feel how hard he was as he pressed himself against her. His hand ran down Abby's naked body and back up, stopping to caress her large soft breasts. His hand continued wandering from her breasts down her stomach and stopped between her legs. He massaged her lips before slipping two of his fingers between them. As his fingers brushed past Abby's clit, she trembled.

"That's what you like, isn't it?" he said as he went right back to the sensitive clump of nerves and began massaging it.

Abby moaned loudly, giving Ryan the answer he was looking for. Ryan forced his index and middle finger inside Abby while his thumb rubbed her clit faster and faster. Her breathing began to get very fast, and her legs shook. She squirmed and tried to escape the overload of pleasure, but Ryan held her against him while she cried out. Suddenly, Ryan could feel Abby's pussy contracting, and her clit throbbed. A splash of moisture made Ryan's hand wet as Abby squirted and moaned his name. Before she could even turn over, Ryan had thrust himself inside her, filling her completely with his girth and length. Abby moaned again as her body stretched to accept him. They humped for a moment side by side until Ryan pushed Abby onto her stomach and rolled on top of her. He lay on her, obviously exhausted too. His weight made his cock press inside her even deeper. Abby wiggled her butt, teasing Ryan a bit. It made him fuck her hard. With how fast and deeply he was thrusting, Ryan filled Abby with his warm fluids within moments. He fell off her satisfied. Normally, Abby would run to the bathroom after sex to clean up, but they were both in a deep state of relaxation. She felt his juices leak out of her when she rolled over but didn't care. Ryan wrapped his arms around her again once she got comfortable, and they both went off to sleep.

Abby woke up thinking it would be dark out if they had gotten at least a couple of hours of sleep. She looked around to see the sun peeking through the curtains. Ryan was still sleeping heavily. She got out of bed and ran to the bathroom. Peeing was a challenge after their activities before bed. She had no complaints though. Once she was done, she looked in the mirror. She needed to go get ready at her place across the hall. Abby quietly went back into Ryan's bedroom and grabbed her clothes from the floor. She put on her shirt and pants too so no one would catch her in the hall undressed. Abby retrieved her apartment key from her jeans pocket and went across the hall. She jumped into the shower and quickly cleaned herself up.

Washing her hair took the most amount of time. Instead of doing her routine of blowing it dry and straightening it afterward, Abby just put her clean wet hair into a long braid and wore it down her one side. She put a towel around herself and picked out some new clothes.

I really haven't had time to do laundry, have I? Abby thought when she realized that all her jeans were dirty. She put on a pair of stretchy black yoga pants and a tank top. "At least it's comfy," she said to herself. She found a leopard print sweater in the back of her closet and put it on and walked across the hall again back to Ryan's place.

Abby could still hear Ryan's shallow snore from the bedroom. She walked out to the kitchen and prepared the coffeepot and switched it on. Ryan's phone was on his coffee table. He must have placed it there when he flung his pants off. It was flashing. Abby walked over and looked. Twelve missed calls from the chief. *Wow,* Abby thought, wondering why he would call so much after giving them some time off to rest. That was when she saw the time. It was 4:00 p.m. the next day. Abby and Ryan had slept for almost a full twenty-four hours.

"Oh shit!" Abby said, rushing into Ryan's room. "Ryan!" she said sharply.

"Huh, yeah?" he said, confused as he woke up.

"We slept for a whole day!" she said as she handed him his phone.

Ryan strained his eyes and looked at his phone. "Oh man," he said. He automatically dialed the chief back and explained to him what had happened. Abby could only hear Ryan's end of the conversation, but it seemed like the chief was just checking on them. Ryan finished his short call. "Thank you, sir. I will. Thank you for understanding, sir. See you later this evening," Ryan said before hanging up his phone. He tossed it to the bottom of his bed and threw himself back down onto his pillow. Abby sat before Ryan on the bed. "The chief wasn't surprised that we passed out. Now that the streets are safer, a lot of his officers are catching up on rest," Ryan explained in between yawns.

"Did you say you're seeing him tonight?" Abby asked, trying to clarify.

"*We* are if you're up to it. He invited us out to dinner," Ryan said.

Abby smiled. "Of course," she said gleefully.

A dinner with her boyfriend's boss, after these events, a normal situation like this one was so rare and exciting. Abby tried to contain her excitement, when she noticed that Ryan fell back into a deep sleep again. She slowly got up from the bed and walked out into the living room. *A dinner,* she thought. *I'm going to need some nicer clothes.* Abby quietly left Ryan's to go get ready and try to turn herself into a normal girlfriend.

Clothing was thrown all around Abby's room. "Yes!" she yelled as she found her one and only dress in the back of her closet. It was a black dress that stopped just above the knee with half sleeves. It was also extremely low cut. Abby picked a nice black lace bra to peak out from the top of her dress. She put her bra and underwear on and put the dress over the bed. Abby spent the next hour painting her toenails and fingernails. She removed the braid from her hair. It left her with wavy curls that she decided to work with, curling the rest of her hair, adding volume and style. She put on mascara and liquid eyeliner to make a cat's-eye. To finish off her face, she put on her favorite pearly shine lip chap and walked back to her bed. She slipped on the dress and paired it with her boots, of course. Abby looked at herself in the mirror once more before going back over to Ryan's. She wanted to make sure she looked okay for their first date as a seemingly normal couple.

When Abby got back into Ryan's apartment and saw the time on his microwave, she realized she had been gone for over an hour. Abby checked Ryan's bedroom to find the bed-ripped apartment and Ryan wasn't there, but there was movement coming from the bathroom. He came out wearing a towel around his waist. A plastic bag covered his bandage on his arm. He must not have wanted to get it redone yet again.

"Wow!" he said in shock at the sight of Abby dressed up. He walked over and kissed her passionately while tracing her large amount of displayed cleavage.

"Your boss will be waiting for us soon," Abby said, giggling.

"I know, but I just want to stay home and wreck you," Ryan joked. Abby nudged him to go get ready. "Fiiine," he said as he went back to his bedroom to get dressed.

Abby waited in the living room, once again looking at the photos of Ryan's family. "Are you mad that we didn't kill him?" Abby asked. This was an answer she was worried about getting. The sound of Ryan's movements paused. "I'm sorry, I shouldn't have said that today," she said quickly, hoping she didn't just ruin their night out.

"No, no," he said, trying to smooth it over. "You caught me off guard, but it's a valid question. No, I'm not. I'm actually happy we did it this way." He continued from his room. Ryan walked out wearing black dress pants, black socks, and a white undershirt. He carried his button-up dress shirt in his hands and placed it over his TV.

"Really? I was worried you would be disappointed," Abby said, looking at Ryan. She sat on his couch.

"I will admit that killing him would have given me closure, but there's hundreds, if not thousands, of other people who suffered in some way because of him. This way, they'll all get closure," he said. Ryan was being so rational. Maybe it was because of all the sleep he had gotten finally.

"Thank you," Abby replied.

Ryan looked at her, puzzled. "Don't second-guess yourself," he said as he walked over and put his hand under Abby's chin. "You saved countless future victims," he said. "That's more than anyone else has been able to do for the last two decades." Ryan continued.

Abby took his hand and held it for a moment. Then she got up and held Ryan's shirt out, guiding his arms into the proper holes.

Ryan and Abby walked through the parking lot and got into his car. The streetlights that weren't smashed were just starting to come on as the sun was leaving for another night. Ryan started to drive.

"Where are we going?" Abby asked, smiling.

"Some new steak house that opened just outside of town," Ryan replied. They drove a couple of blocks, and Ryan pulled off onto the side of the road. "I just have to make a quick stop," he said, undoing his seat belt and leaning over to kiss Abby.

Ryan got out and bolted into a small store. Abby looked around. After everything they had been through, it was odd for her to just sit there just a normal girl going out with her man. Odd but not in a bad way at all. Ryan came back quickly and got in the car. Right away, he handed Abby a dozen long stem roses.

"Oh wow!" Abby said, reaching out and accepting them. "This is why you stopped?" she said happily.

"Yes, and these," Ryan said as he pulled out a small package of cigars from his jacket pocket. "The chief loves them." He continued.

"You're just pure class, aren't you?" Abby said flirtatiously.

"You know it," Ryan replied with humor.

Ryan put the car back into drive, and they carried on to meet Chief Doyle. As they drove, Abby kept smelling the fresh cut roses. She never thought she would go from smelling death to smelling roses within days. Abby hoped this was her future because she never wanted this moment to end.

Chapter 19

The restaurant was, in fact, just outside of town like Ryan said. There was plenty of parking in the fields around the country-style steak house. A local farmer ran it, and all the food was grown and butchered locally as well. They walked in and were greeted immediately by a hostess.

"Table for two?" she asked with a smile.

"Actually, we're meeting the chief of police here," Ryan replied.

"Oh, of course. We have a private table in our VIP section," the hostess replied.

Ryan and Abby followed through the restaurant and toward the back. There were glass doors blocking off the VIP section. Ryan opened the door and let Abby and then the hostess go through first. Chief Doyle was already there and going to town on the bread for the table. The rest of the VIP area was completely empty.

"I ordered some appetizers!" the chief yelled in their directions. Ryan and Abby walked over and joined the chief.

"Your waitress will be over shortly. Can I get you started with a drink?" the hostess asked.

"Just water for me," Abby said.

The hostess nodded and looked to Ryan. "I'll have a coffee," he decided.

"I'll be right back with that," the hostess said as she jetted away to grab their drink order.

"How did you find this place?" Abby asked.

"I grew up with the owner. Our farms shared a border," Chief Doyle replied.

"You were a farmer, sir?" Ryan asked, surprised.

"No, no, my father was the farmer. I was running around, arresting chickens. Always wanted to be a lawman," Chief Doyle replied with a look of nostalgia on his face.

The trio stopped talking and looked up as the hostess came and set down the drinks Ryan and Abby ordered.

"Thank you," Abby said as she took a sip of her ice water. Ryan fixed his coffee the way he liked it and stirred it.

"What do you think? Three of their famous twelve-ounce steaks?" Chief Doyle asked with excitement.

"I'm in!" Abby yelled.

"Red meat, I'm in too." Ryan settled it. They all agreed.

Chief Doyle flagged down their waitress and ordered for all three of them. "Now let's do some shoptalk before the meat comes, shall we?" the chief said, placing down papers in front of Abby and Ryan.

"What's this?" Ryan asked as he picked the papers with one hand and sipped his coffee with his other hand.

Ryan flipped through the papers. All had photographs of Abby on them. The photos were taken from a distance and in public places, until they got to the last one. It was a picture of Abby in her living room stretching, taking through her window.

"These were found in Phil Deeks's desk. Looks like he had been keeping surveillance on you for a while," Chief Doyle said.

"And to think I almost felt bad for the way he died," Ryan said.

"Our coroner took a while to identify him. There wasn't much left," Chief Doyle said with no remorse. He had lost a lot of good men. Losing a bad one wasn't much of his concern.

"I don't mean to be rude," Abby said. "But why are you showing me this now?" she asked. Ryan nodded in agreement with Abby's question.

"My fear is that he wasn't the only one watching you because of what you can do. And now that we know you were watched in your own home, it would be a smart idea to think about moving," Chief Doyle said bluntly but with concern for her safety.

Ryan smiled and looked at Abby. "You mean somewhere with no windows? Because it's way below our feet?" Ryan commented.

Abby smiled. "You guys are going to let me have the room Alexander showed me?" Abby said as she bounced a little in her chair.

"It does make sense safety-wise. And you can keep the hounds down there too," Ryan said to Abby, touching her leg.

"You can't have the four back that you lent us yet," Chief Doyle joked. "Alexander's bail hearing will be tomorrow morning. Bail is definitely going to be rejected, and our courts are backed up. I'm hoping they give him a closer trial date considering his crimes," Chief Doyle explained.

The conversation was interrupted as the waitress brought over the three steaks. They completely covered the large dinner plates and didn't have fat on them, just pure thick cuts of meat. Abby cut into her steak and took a bite. It was the best steak she'd ever tried. *If people were meant to be vegetarians, then why is steak so good?* Abby thought. Ryan and Chief Doyle kept talking about the upcoming trial. Abby pretended she was listening, but the steak paired with the knowledge that she was moving was sending her into pleasure overload. Abby dropped a small piece of meat down her shirt, and it rested on her displayed cleavage.

"Goal!" she said, and she picked it off her. The chief and Ryan both laughed, and Abby finally joined back into the conversation. "Has he tried to escape yet?" Abby asked, regarding Alexander.

"God, no." Chief Doyle laughed. "Anytime he ever moves to use the toilet in there, the hounds are growling and acting like they want to eat him," the chief said.

Abby smiled. The thought of Alexander getting eaten wasn't a bad thought at all. No one deserved that fate more than him. "Puppies," Abby said, thinking about her loyal beasts.

"Yeah . . . puppies," Ryan said sarcastically. He and the chief laughed a bit. Their idea of puppies was a very different one.

"How is everything?" a waitress said from out of nowhere.

Abby and Ryan were visibly startled. "You sneaked up on us." Ryan laughed.

"Sorry! Is there anything else I can get you?" she asked.

"Nope, I think we're good with our giant slabs of meat," the chief joked.

The waitress smiled and left, closing the glass doors behind her. Abby focused on her half-eaten steak and thought she was eating too fast. She looked at Chief Doyle's and Ryan's plates. They were almost done. She didn't feel so bad now and decided to finish up. The glass doors opened once again, and a large jolly-looking man with an apron came in smiling.

"Ben!" Chief Doyle yelled.

"Charles! It's so good to see you, man!" he replied.

That was the first time Abby had ever heard anyone call the chief by his first name. The pair hugged.

"This is the owner of this fine establishment," Chief Doyle said with his arm around his lifelong friend.

Ben smiled at Abby and Ryan and enjoyed seeing how much they liked his food. "You guys are at the old station just up the road now, eh?" Ben asked his guests. "About five minutes down the highway on the edge of town." The two old men talked as they caught up after many years. "We're opening up a new bar side, so if you guys are even looking for a new cop hangout, I can offer a special law enforcement tab," Ben said, winking at his old friend.

"Now that sounds like a plan," Chief Doyle said.

They high-fived right before a woman cracked open the door to tell Ben he was needed in the kitchen.

"Ah, well, duty calls. Your steaks are on the house by the way," he said as he walked toward the door.

"You don't have to do that!" Ryan said after stuffing the last piece of his steak into his mouth.

"Nonsense," Ben replied. "Words getting around, and if it wasn't for the arrest you guys made, I wouldn't have any customers tonight anyway," Ben said as he rushed back to the kitchen.

"Has curfew been canceled?" Abby asked.

Ryan looked to the chief since he wasn't sure. "It hasn't officially been canceled, but it's not being enforced right now. Tomorrow afternoon, I have a press conference," he replied.

Abby finished her steak and took a deep breath. She was so stuffed. All those times she had said that she was so hungry she could eat a cow, she didn't realize how wrong she was. Eating twelve ounces of cow was hard enough. Chief Doyle sat and cleared his plate.

"Dessert anyone?" he asked.

Ryan and Abby looked at him. "Really?" they both said at the same time. All three of them laughed.

"I'm too full, but I'm having a good time here," Abby said. Ryan looked at her and smiled. They held hands under the table.

"Then I'm ordering pie, and the good times can last even longer," the chief said happily.

The chief went and spoke to a waitress who was right outside the VIP doors. She went to the back right away. Chief Doyle walked back in and sat again.

"I just need to go use the washroom," Abby said.

She got up, and both the gentlemen at her table rose with her. Ryan kissed her on the cheek, and she walked out of the VIP area. Abby stopped and looked around until she saw a sign for the washroom. She walked through the restaurant to the front and into the bathroom to do her thing that was just inside the entrance. As she came out, she saw someone familiar staring at her through the window from outside. It was Stephen, the only man of Alexander whom Abby let go. Abby went outside and greeted him.

"Stephen? What are you doing here?" she asked. She shivered and held her hands together.

"You told me to find you if I wanted a job," he said. "I was worried you were like your brother, but you let me go. He would have never done that," Stephen explained.

"Come inside. It's freezing out here tonight," Abby said.

They came inside, and the light made it clear that Stephen had been on the run since they last saw each other. His eyes were darkened, and his clothing was dirty.

"Would you be willing to testify for the chief of police against your old boss?" Abby asked. Stephen looked scared at this thought. "He's here now, and if I introduce you, I'm sure we can all come to some sort of understanding," Abby explained.

"I don't mind if I have to go to jail. But I don't want to be in the same jail as Alexander. I'd be dead within an hour," Stephen said with his voice coated in fear.

"That's not going to happen. He's in an empty jail now as it is," Abby explained.

Stephen reluctantly agreed to come speak to the chief. They walked to the back of the restaurant and went through the large glass doors. Ryan and Chief Doyle looked up in confusion at the new guest Abby brought.

"Chief Doyle, this is Stephen," she said.

The chief stood and walked around the table to shake his hand. Ryan sat in his chair, waiting to find out who this one was.

"Stephen used to work for Alexander. He would like to help us put him away after witnessing the things he did. And experiencing them, right?" Abby said.

Stephen looked at her, not too surprised that she was able to see into his head since he already dealt with her much darker sibling. "He killed my family, it destroyed me, and I had no direction. I've finally found that direction again," Stephen said, pleading his case.

"I'm inclined to believe Ms. Briggs on these things," Chief Doyle said, smiling at Abby. "Why don't we order some more pie and talk about everything you witnessed? Would that be okay, son?" Chief Doyle said.

Abby and Ryan got themselves ready and decided to give Chief Doyle and his new witness some time and space to debrief each other. Ryan ordered some pie to go after seeing how good the chief's piece looked. They left and headed to the car that they parked way out in the open field. Abby was glad she wore her boots. The grass was so long, and she hated mosquito bites.

"Wait!" a voice shouted. Chief Doyle was rushing out carrying Ryan's phone that he had forgotten on the table.

"Thank you so much, sir," Ryan said, reaching into his jacket, putting away his phone. He felt something in his pocket and remembered. "Before I forget again, Chief, these are for you," Ryan said, handing the chief the package of cigars he had purchased when he stopped on the way there.

"Thank you, son," he said as they shook hands. "I'll see you at the station tomorrow?" the chief said.

Ryan answered, "Of course, sir."

Chief Doyle looked to Abby next. "And what about you? Will I be seeing you tomorrow?" he asked Abby.

Abby looked confused at his words. "Is that a job offer?" Abby joked. "Because I am unemployed after my place of employment burned to hell," she added.

"Then that settles it. I'll see my power team in the morning," the chief said, hitting them both on the back playfully.

Ryan and Abby got in the car and turned it on to heat it up. "What just happened?" Abby said.

"Looks like I finally got a partner I can trust," Ryan said with a giant smile on his face.

Abby picked the flowers she had left on the dashboard and put them on her lap. The whole car smelled like roses now. Ryan drove home with a huge smile, and Abby was almost too excited to talk. The thought of working with Ryan each day was awesome, and now she could move into her new place below the Townsquare building tomorrow afternoon after they dealt with Alexander's bail hearing. Abby didn't even notice the time went by. Ryan pulled into the parking lot of their current building and parked.

"I guess you'll be packing what you want, eh?" he asked.

"Only my personal items. The furniture there was so much nicer. And the bed, wait until you feel it," Abby said, flirting.

"I'll leave my door unlocked for you to come over when you're done," Ryan said.

"Actually, I was going to pack and spend one last night there if that's okay," Abby requested.

"Of course, I didn't mean to assume," he replied. They walked into the building hand in hand. "I'll come knocking around eight thirty for work," Ryan said as they embraced each other in the hallway between their apartments.

"I'll be ready to go then," Abby said before Ryan kissed her.

"I love you, Abby," he said, looking into her eyes.

"I love you too," she said as she kissed him back.

Ryan ran his hand down Abby's arm when they turned to unlock their separate doors. They both looked back and smiled at each other before saying good night and going to their own apartments.

Abby sat on her bed and kicked off her boots. She didn't have much to pack, just some clothes. Most of her stuff was still in boxes. Since they never felt at home, she never unpacked. Abby noticed something unusual, a dusty box with a ribbon around it on her couch. It wasn't there before. A noise came from the box when Abby touched it. Abby undid the ribbon slowly, and before she could open the lid, a small fury head popped out. It was a feline-looking version of the hellhounds Abby had already grown to love. Its eyes were tinted red, and its fur was rough and thick as well. It was as black as coal too. Two small fangs hung out over its lip. There was a small note inside the box that Abby grabbed and read as she held the tiny beast.

> *This is Hecate.*
> *She is just as special as you.*
> *You will need each other.*

Abby flipped the note over, looking for more or to see who it was from. It was blank other than those words. Abby looked at her new friend. Hecate meowed and purred as Abby petted her like any other cat. Abby looked around, and there wasn't anyone in the apartment.

Whoever left her had come and gone through a locked door, like they appeared and vanished in thin hair. Abby tossed the box down, aggravating some of the dust on the box and in the area. It had been over a week since she cleaned. The dust went up in both their faces. Abby coughed a bit and tried blowing the dust away from them. Hecate breathed in some of the dust and sneezed. A small flame shot out of her mouth but dissipated before it landed anywhere to start a fire. Dark smoke circled the kitten's head. Abby laughed and picked her new friend.

"Now I see why we we're put together."

The end. For now.

Abby will be back in another action-packed adventure to wrap up the trial of Alexander with more murder, sex, and monsters!

Printed in the United States
By Bookmasters